Cupcakes Are Forever

The Cupcake Club

Also by Sheryl Berk and Carrie Berk

The Cupcake Club Series

Peace, Love, and Cupcakes

Recipe for Trouble

Winner Bakes All

Icing on the Cake

Baby Cakes

Royal Icing

Sugar and Spice

Sweet Victory

Bakers on Board

Vote for Cupcakes!

Hugs and Sprinkles

Fashion Academy Series

Fashion Academy

Runway Ready

Designer Drama

Model Madness

Fashion Face-Off

Cupcakes Are Forever

The Cupcake Club

Sheryl Berk and Carrie Berk

sourcebooks
jabberwocky

Published by Sourcebooks Jabberwocky, an imprint of Sourcebooks, Inc.
P.O. Box 4410, Naperville, Illinois 60567-4410
(630) 961-3900
Fax: (630) 961-2168
www.sourcebooks.com

Library of Congress Cataloging-in-Publication Data

Names: Berk, Sheryl, author. | Berk, Carrie, illustrator.
Title: Cupcakes are forever / Sheryl Berk and Carrie Berk.
Description: Naperville, Illinois : Sourcebooks Jabberwocky, [2017] | Series:
    The Cupcake Club ; 12 | Summary: The girls of Peace, Love, and Cupcakes
    are feeling sentimental about the end of elementary school, especially
    after Principal Fontina asks Kylie to create a PLC junior club to live on
    at Blakely.
Identifiers: LCCN 2017017032 | (alk. paper)
Subjects: | CYAC: Clubs--Fiction. | Friendship--Fiction. | Graduation
    (School)--Fiction. | Schools--Fiction. | Cupcakes--Fiction. |
    Baking--Fiction.
Classification: LCC PZ7.B45236 Cv 2017 | DDC [Fic]--dc23 LC record
available at https://lccn.loc.gov/2017017032

Source of Production: Versa Press, East Peoria, Illinois, USA
Date of Production: August 2017
Run Number: 5010253

Printed and bound in the United States of America.
VP 10 9 8 7 6 5 4 3 2 1

To all our loyal PLC fans. Thank you for making this such a sweet journey.

Hooray for Monday!

Kylie Carson jumped out of bed minutes before her alarm rang. How could she sleep when she was so excited to get to school this morning?

Her mom peeked into her bedroom, surprised to find Kylie already dressed and ready to go. "Well, someone's up bright and early!"

"You know what day today is?" Kylie asked her.

"Let's see," her mom replied. "Monday, April 6?"

"Yes…but something even better than that!"

"The start of the new season of *Cake Boss* on TV?"

Kylie paused to consider. "Nope, that's next week. Guess again."

"The first day you'll make your bed without me having to ask you?"

Kylie quickly pulled up her purple comforter and fluffed the pillows. "Nice try. Keep guessing."

"I give up," Mrs. Carson said. "What is today?"

"Assembly Day!"

Her mom raised an eyebrow. "Assembly Day? The day you always complain about because it's—and I quote— *sooooo* boring?"

"Well, today's assembly is different," Kylie insisted. "First period, Principal Fontina is going to tell the fifth grade all about graduation!"

"Oh." Mrs. Carson smiled. "I see."

"Can you believe it, Mom? I'm graduating from elementary school six weeks from today!"

Her mom sighed. "No, I can't believe it. It seems like just yesterday you were the new kid in fourth grade, and I was dragging you out of bed so you wouldn't be late for Ms. Shottlan's class."

Kylie sighed. "Oh, yeah. My monster movies presentation. I remember that!"

"I also remember how nervous you were that you would never make any friends—and look at you now, president of Peace, Love, and Cupcakes."

"I guess I have come a long way, haven't I?" Kylie considered. "And next year is only going to be bigger and better. Jenna, Sadie, Lexi, Delaney, and I have lots of plans for our cupcake club in middle school."

"I bet you do," her mom said. "And I can't wait to hear all about them—and the details of graduation. Make sure you take lots of notes."

"I will," Kylie said, kissing her mom good-bye and heading to the school bus stop.

☆ ☮ ☆

When she arrived at Blakely Elementary, her best friends had already saved her a seat in the front row of the auditorium.

"Kylie, over here!" Lexi waved when she spotted her. "Hurry!"

Kylie chuckled to herself. She remembered how Lexi used to be so painfully shy. Now she was shouting and practically standing on her seat trying to get Kylie's attention.

"*Chica*, we saved you a place of honor—next to me," Jenna teased and moved her backpack so Kylie could sit down.

"Thanks," Kylie said. "Did I miss anything?"

"Only Jenna complaining that she's starving." Lexi giggled.

"I only had one blueberry pancake for breakfast," Jenna explained. "My siblings stole the whole stack before I could have any more."

"You have to be quicker," Sadie advised her. "My two bros never beat me to the pancakes because I've mastered the grab-and-gobble technique." She mimed how she swooped in over their heads and lifted a pancake off the pile. "It's like a hook shot in basketball."

"I don't play basketball," Jenna said. "And you haven't seen Ricky and Manny in action at the breakfast table. Those twins are like vultures."

Kylie squirmed in her seat. "I wish the assembly would start already." She saw that Principal Fontina was fussing with the projection screen. "I mean, what's she waiting for?"

"What's the big rush?" Lexi asked.

"Nothing," Kylie said, shrugging. "I'm just excited, that's all. I mean, middle school is just around the corner. Graduation is just around the corner."

"I'm not so eager to graduate," Jenna piped up. "I like it here. I've been here since pre-K, six years. Why would I want to leave?"

"Yeah, I kind of agree," Sadie said. "I love the basketball court and the bleachers and my gym locker."

"That's 'cause you've covered it with New England Patriots stickers," Jenna said. "Like wallpapered the entire locker."

"I can't help it," Sadie said. "They're my favorite football team. Go, Pats!"

"I'll miss the art studio," Lexi reflected. "And of course the kitchen in the Blakely teachers' lounge where we started PLC. How about you, Kylie? What will you miss?"

Kylie sighed. "I'd rather not think about it. I don't want to be stuck in the past."

"It's not being stuck… It's being nostalgic," Lexi corrected her. "Or sentimental. I'm going to walk around with my sketchbook and draw every detail of Blakely so I don't forget it."

"Ooh, can you make me a drawing of the cafeteria?" Jenna asked her. "I don't ever wanna forget cheese fries Fridays. They're my fave."

"You talk like we'll never be here again, like we'll never see Blakely," Kylie pointed out. "Bynder Middle School is only three blocks away, just down the road."

"Yeah, but we'll be sixth graders," Sadie pointed out. "With lots more homework and responsibility. Who knows if we'll have any time to come back."

"Well, even if we're not here, Herbie will be," Kylie said, pointing out the cupcake club's adviser and resident robotics expert onstage. He was helping Principal Fontina start her PowerPoint presentation on her laptop.

"Excited, ladies?" a voice asked from the aisle. It was Ms. Shottlan, Kylie's fourth-grade teacher.

"Very!" Kylie exclaimed. At last, *someone* who understood how she was feeling.

"Graduation is a very special time—a time for endings and beginnings. You might feel a little sad when you start thinking about leaving Blakely, but that's perfectly normal."

Not her too! "I'm not sad," Kylie said. "Not at all."

Ms. Shottlan looked puzzled. "Okay, I'm glad to hear it. I just thought for you especially, Kylie, leaving Blakely would be tough. It's where you made your best friends and started your whole cupcaking adventure."

"Well, the adventure isn't over," Kylie said stubbornly. "I don't get why everyone is so 'Boo-hoo, I'll miss Blakely.'"

"She's in denial," Jenna whispered to Ms. Shottlan.

"I'm not!" Kylie said, overhearing her. "I'm just saying that I'm excited about all the possibilities. There's so much more I want to do!"

"Good for you," Ms. Shottlan said. "But I personally will miss you all dearly."

Lexi stood up and gave her teacher a hug. "I'm sorry about the time I threw up on you during my second-grade Picasso oral report," she apologized.

"Oh, don't be silly! You've grown up so much since then," Ms. Shottlan said. "I'm so proud of you. Of all of you."

Principal Fontina suddenly bellowed into the microphone. "Attention! Attention, fifth graders, we're ready to begin."

Finally! Kylie sat up tall in her seat and tried to tune out all the chatter around her.

"Good morning, Blakely students," Principal Fontina said.

"Good morning, Principal Fontina!" the audience replied in unison.

"Today is a very special assembly…as I'm sure you're all aware." Herbie hit a button on the computer, and a picture of a graduation cap and diploma popped up on the screen. "We are talking today about graduation—the ceremony as well as what it means for every one of you."

"I think I'm gonna cry," Lexi said, grabbing Kylie's arm. "I can't believe this is actually happening."

Kylie rolled her eyes. If her BFF was going to sniffle and sob through the entire assembly, she'd never be able to hear Principal Fontina!

"Graduation will take place exactly six weeks from today," their principal continued. "It's a big day for you, one that's filled with many emotions. I know you have lots of questions."

"I wanna know what they're serving at the graduation reception," Jenna whispered to her friends. "I heard it's a brunch buffet."

"Let me go through all the details, and then I'll open the floor up for anything you'd like to ask," Principal Fontina continued. "We have a lot of ground to cover."

Over the next forty-five minutes, she outlined everything that would happen on Graduation Day, from the songs the fifth grade would be singing, to the color of their caps and gowns—blue and gold. The morning ceremony would be about two hours long and would include commencement addresses by two fifth graders. "We will choose the speakers based on an essay contest," Principal Fontina explained. "You will submit five hundred words on the topic 'What Blakely means to me.'"

"OMG, an essay?" Sadie gasped. "I hate writing essays. I'm terrible at them."

"I'll help you," Lexi assured her. "You just have to plan it out and make sure you have a strong conclusion."

"I always say way too much…kind of like how I talk," Jenna added. "I don't think five hundred words will be enough."

"Starting this week, there will be graduation rehearsal every Wednesday morning," Principal Fontina said. "We will practice every detail till it's smooth as silk."

"Or smooth as our buttercream frosting," Lexi whispered.

"I have hired a special graduation coordinator who will oversee the entire production from start to finish." Principal Fontina leaned forward at her podium. "Are there any questions?"

A hand shot up from the corner of the auditorium.

"Will there be a graduation dance?" It was Meredith Mitchell, Blakely's resident queen bee. Kylie knew she would definitely *not* miss Meredith. The rumor was that Mr. and Mrs. Mitchell were sending their darling daughter to a posh boarding school next year in Switzerland! Meredith had bullied Kylie from the moment she arrived at Blakely and for no good reason. During a hip-hop club audition, Kylie had accidentally kicked off her sneaker, and it gave Meredith a black eye. Meredith had vowed revenge—and nearly destroyed PLC just when the club was getting started. Thankfully, Ms. Shottlan had stepped in to referee, and things had quieted down between them in fifth grade. But that didn't mean that Meredith was any less stuck-up or annoying.

"I mean, most schools have a prom—with music and lights and gorgeous gowns." Meredith was elaborating. "Oh, and a prom queen with a huge crown!"

"There will be a dance," Principal Fontina assured her. "At night in the school gymnasium."

Meredith's hand went up again. "Will there be a dance committee…and someone to head it who will make it the social event of the year?"

Principal Fontina sighed. "I suppose that would be a good idea. Are you volunteering to chair the committee, Meredith?"

Meredith smiled wide. "Me? Chair the dance committee? If you insist!"

Jenna pretended to gag. "Great. Our graduation dance is gonna turn into a Meredith 'Me, me, me, I love me' party."

Principal Fontina fielded a few more questions, then closed her laptop. "Have a great Monday, and you're all dismissed…except for Kylie Carson. Please see me in my office immediately."

PLC Jr.

Kylie waited nervously on the bench outside Principal Fontina's office. What had she done wrong? Had the principal noticed Kylie rolling her eyes during assembly? Or worse, had Ms. Shottlan ratted her out for not being upset about leaving Blakely?

The door suddenly opened. "Come in, Kylie," Principal Fontina said. "Take a seat."

She pointed to a chair across from her desk. "I suppose you know why I've called you here this morning."

"I'm sorry," Kylie said. "I didn't mean to be disrespectful."

Principal Fontina raised an eyebrow. "Am I missing something?"

Kylie bit her lip. "I'm not in trouble? For telling Ms. Shottlan I wasn't sad?"

"Sad? Why would you be sad?"

"Well, everyone seems to be really upset about graduating. I'm just not. I can't wait to get to middle school!"

"Well, I commend your enthusiasm," Principal Fontina said. "But I do hope you'll miss your old school—and your old principal—just a little."

"Of course I will," Kylie said. "But I choose to look on the bright side…toward the future."

"Good." Principal Fontina smiled. "I'm happy you feel that way. Because I have a task for you that involves just that…the future of your club here at Blakely."

Kylie looked confused. "PLC? What about it?"

"I know it's become a thriving business for you and your friends, but I'd love to continue a cupcake club here at our school—a Peace, Love, and Cupcakes Jr., so to speak. You can pick the members and train them yourself. And I think a great first assignment would be to bake cupcakes for the graduation reception. Five hundred cupcakes for the students and guests would do it—and a wonderful centerpiece to display them. The new junior members can pitch in, and Herbie can continue supervising them next year."

Kylie's jaw dropped. Five hundred cupcakes was a big order, but that wasn't the problem. Was Principal Fontina actually telling her to hand over her club to a bunch of inexperienced elementary schoolers? To turn over everything she had worked so hard to create to kids who knew *nothing* about baking, frosting, and decorating delicious cupcakes?

"Um, I'm not so sure about that," she began. "I mean, it takes a very special person to be a member of PLC…"

Principal Fontina interrupted her. "Which is why I am entrusting you to pick your successors here at Blakely. You, Jenna, Sadie, Lexi, and your friend Delaney in her school… You can each choose someone and take them under your wing."

She ushered Kylie out the door of her office. "Have a great Monday!"

☆ ☮ ☆

"Why the long face?" Sadie asked, catching up to Kylie in the hallway. "I thought you were the only one around here who wasn't sad. Wait. Did Principal Fontina yell at you for rolling your eyes during her presentation?"

"Nuh-uh," Kylie replied. "Worse."

"Worse?" Sadie asked. "Is she calling your parents? Writing a note on your permanent record?"

Kylie shook her head. "Even worse than that. She's making me start a new cupcake club with a bunch of munchkins!"

Sadie scratched her head. "Okay, that makes no sense.

First off, it's our business, and second, munchkins are imaginary little people from Oz, right?"

"Right! I mean wrong!" Kylie was getting exasperated. "She wants us to start a junior PLC here at Blakely so they can learn from us. We're supposed to take a bunch of kids under our wing."

Sadie considered for a moment. "Well, is that really such a bad thing? I mean, think of how much being a member of the club meant for each of us. It changed our lives."

"Yes, *our* lives," Kylie insisted. "PLC belongs to us."

"Think of it as branching out," Sadie said. "Inspiring the youth of tomorrow."

Kylie groaned. "Okay, now you sound like Principal Fontina."

"It's like when I'm running track and I pass the baton to one of my teammates," Sadie tried to explain. "Couldn't we pass the baton to a few kids who need some cupcakes and confidence in their lives?"

Kylie sighed. Now Sadie was making her feel guilty. "You're saying we pick a few kids who need PLC in their lives."

"Exactly! Think of how shy Lexi was, how left out Jenna felt, how unsure I was, how alone you were. But together, as a club, we became an unstoppable force!"

Kylie smiled recalling the day in fourth grade they had all met for PLC's first meeting. Each of them was an outsider, a misfit, a loner in her own way. And their first bake had been a total disaster, with flour flying and cupcakes hard as hockey pucks. But once they took their time and learned to work together, Sadie was right—they were a force to be reckoned with.

"Do you think there are kids at Blakely who need PLC as badly as we did?" Kylie asked.

"Of course! We won't have any trouble finding them," Sadie said. "Who wouldn't want to join the coolest club at Blakely?" Out of the corner of her eye, she spied a little girl strolling down the hall, juggling bright-yellow tennis balls. As she walked past the lockers, other students pointed, laughed, and whispered. "Don't look now, but I think I see our first potential member."

Kylie studied the girl. She was small with two red pigtails that stuck out just above her ears. She reminded Kylie of Juliette, PLC's first adviser and Blakely's former drama teacher. When Kylie was feeling picked on by Meredith and her posse, Juliette had confided in her that she had also been bullied when she was a kid—for having hair the color of red velvet cupcakes. She inspired Kylie to start the club. Without Juliette, there would be no PLC. And Kylie knew exactly what Juliette would advise her to do if she were still here…

"Fine, you win," she told Sadie. "Let's go recruit her."

The girl had three balls in the air when Kylie called to her. "Hey, you!"

The juggler was so startled that she nearly dropped two of the balls. "Me?" The girl looked around. Why would a fifth grader be speaking to her, a measly third grader? Unless they were going to pick on her, like almost everyone else did? She did an about-face and began to walk quickly away.

"Wait!" Sadie shouted. "We want to talk to you! We think you've got some serious skills."

The girl stopped in her tracks. "Skills? I'm not really very good at anything."

"Really? You could have fooled me. You're an amazing juggler!" Kylie said.

"Oh, that," the girl replied. "I know it's silly…"

"No! It's awesome," Sadie insisted. "Why would you think it's silly?"

"Because everyone in third grade thinks it is," she said. "They think I'm a weirdo. They call me Clementine the

Clown. But I'll show them. One day, I'm gonna win *America's Got Talent* or break the world record for most balls juggled."

"Well, we don't think you're a weirdo," Kylie said, putting an arm around her. "You're just different, and that's what makes you special."

"Yeah, we all started out with people thinking we were weird," Sadie added. "And look at us now."

Clementine looked her up, then down. "You're really tall," she told Sadie. "Like a giant."

Kylie giggled. "A giant with a giant talent. Nobody cracks eggs like Sadie. She's a master cupcake baker."

Clementine's eyes grew wide. "Wait. Are you those cupcake girls?" she asked.

Kylie smiled proudly. "That would be us: Peace, Love, and Cupcakes."

"Well, just so you know, I have lots of food allergies, and my mom said I can't have your cupcakes because you bake with nuts."

"Oh," Kylie said. "So you're allergic to all those things?"

Clementine nodded. "My face gets all red and blotchy, and my lips swell up like balloons. I have to sit at the allergy table at lunch."

"Wow," Sadie remarked. "That's not fun."

"No, it isn't," Clementine said in a huff. "So please keep your cupcakes far away from me." Once again, she turned and walked away.

"So *that* went well," Kylie said sarcastically. "And you thought this would be easy?"

"Patience is a virtue. At least that's what my mom always says," Sadie reminded her. "And I'm not giving up on Clementine just yet. If you recall, you had to do a lot of convincing to get all of us to join PLC."

Kylie did remember handing out flyers and putting up posters—even approaching Jenna in the schoolyard and presenting her with her best sales pitch.

"Fine, I'll give it to the end of the week," she replied.

"And I'll get Jenna, Lexi, and Delaney onboard to help us find members," Sadie said. "Just think, before long we'll have a whole new cupcake club starting up!"

Kylie did think about it…and it gave her a sinking feeling in the pit of her stomach.

Mini-Me's

"Let me get this straight," Jenna said, taking a bite out of her burger at the lunch table. "I'm supposed to find a clone of myself?"

"Sorta." Sadie tried to explain. "Someone you feel has PLC potential and might be able to do what you do."

"*No es posible*," Jenna said, heaping a pile of onions, ketchup, relish, and mustard on her burger.

"You see?" Kylie jumped in. "Jenna thinks it's a bad idea too."

"I didn't say that." Jenna corrected her. "I said it was impossible. I'm one of a kind. No one can live up to this fabulosity!"

Sadie laughed. "True, but maybe you can find a close second."

"Maybe," Jenna agreed. "After I get some pickles. A burger without a pickle is like a cupcake without frosting."

She reached for a pickle on Lexi's plate, but Lexi slapped her hand.

"Hey! Get your own!" she said.

"Fine, fine," Jenna said, getting up from her seat and heading for the toppings bar. She saw another girl she didn't know picking at the platter of pickle chips.

"Hey," Jenna warned her. "Save some of those for the rest of the fifth grade, *por favor.*"

"I'm in the fourth grade," the girl replied. "I was here first. You snooze, you lose." She grabbed the last two chips and popped them in her mouth.

"Thanks," Jenna shot back. "You just ruined my lunch."

"*Adiós!*" the girl said, racing off before Jenna could say another word.

Jenna returned to the table empty-handed.

"Where are your pickles?" Lexi asked her.

"Stolen…by some mouthy fourth grader," Jenna said, sighing. "She's got some nerve."

"Nerve?" Sadie said, raising an eyebrow. "And mouthy. Sound like anyone you know?"

Jenna looked across the cafeteria. The girl was sitting by herself at a back table—just like she used to do before she met her PLC besties. Jenna reached across the table and grabbed some pickles off Lexi's plate.

"Those are mine!" Lexi protested.

"I know, but I need them," Jenna told her. And with that, she took her tray and walked over to join the girl at her table.

"Great, so now you're going to yell at me?" the girl asked her.

"I'm not going to yell," Jenna said, handing her the stash she had taken from Lexi. "I come bearing a pickle peace offering."

"Oh," the girl said.

"That's it? Just 'oh'? The term is '*de nada*' or 'thank you.'"

"I know what '*de nada*' means," the girl replied. "My mom teaches Spanish at Bynder Middle School."

"*Sí?*" Jenna asked. "Then I suppose you know what '*Está ocupada esta silla?*' means."

The girl nodded. "Yeah. I mean, no! This seat isn't taken." She moved over and made space for Jenna to join her. After all, she *had* brought more pickles.

Jenna looked over the other girl's plate. "You like a lot of stuff on your burger, don't you?" she asked.

"Tomato, cheese, onions, lettuce, ketchup, mustard…"

the girl replied. "And of course pickles. A burger without pickles is like a cake without frosting."

Jenna's jaw dropped. "That's exactly how I feel. Why would anyone ever eat a naked cupcake or a naked burger if they could avoid it?"

The girl nodded. "It makes no sense."

Jenna held out her hand. "I'm Jenna Medina. And you are?"

"Starving," the girl said. "Can we maybe eat more, talk less? I have to get back to my class library period before they notice I'm missing. I was just so hungry that I couldn't wait for my class to go to lunch."

"I hear ya," Jenna said. "But maybe we could talk another time…about my club."

"Your club?" the girl asked, her mouth full.

"Peace, Love, and Cupcakes," Jenna continued. "We're starting a junior club here at Blakely that will continue after my friends and I graduate. Maybe you could be in it."

The girl wiped her mouth with a napkin. "Why?"

"I dunno," Jenna said. "Because you remind me of me when I was in fourth grade. I didn't have a lot of friends, and I felt like an outsider."

"Well, for your information, I don't need friends."

Jenna realized the girl was trying to sound tough. She had done the same thing in the past, putting up a wall that no one was able to get through.

"It's up to you," Jenna said. "But in the meantime…" She dug in her jacket pocket and pulled out a snack pack of Oreo cookies. "I carry these with me at all times…in case of a munchy emergency. Ya never know."

The girl nodded. "Double Stuf. My favorite."

Jenna smiled. "So now you owe me pickles *and* a pack of Oreos. Whatever your name is."

"Roxy," the girl said. "It's really Roxanne, but that's what my mom calls me."

"Nice to meet you, Roxy or Roxanne. And PLC meets every Wednesday after school."

Kylie made sure she put out several extra seats around the kitchen table in the teachers' lounge—in case a bunch of students showed up for the first meeting of PLC Jr. She'd made colorful flyers and stuffed them into practically every locker in the school. But as the clock ticked close to three thirty, the start time for the meeting, there was no one in the room but her.

"Let's get this party started!" Delaney said, bursting through the door. A little girl with bouncy auburn curls and dressed in a pink ruffled dress was trailing behind her.

"Kylie, meet Whitney," Delaney announced. "She's in third grade at Weber Day School…"

"And I had the lead in the elementary school musical," Whitney volunteered. "I was Annie in *Annie*."

"Of course you were," Kylie said, trying to be polite. "And do you like to bake?"

"No, not really," Whitney replied.

"Whit, we discussed this, didn't we?" Delaney said through gritted teeth. "We are going to *act* like we like to bake."

"Oh right, sorry," the girl said. She smiled brightly and pulled a frilly apron out of her backpack.

"She came with a costume… I love it," Delaney said.

"And I *love* to bake!" Whitney chirped. "Was that good? Too much? I could try my line again."

Kylie frowned. "This is your candidate for the junior cupcake club?" she whispered to Delaney.

"You said to find someone I could train, and Whitney has star potential," Delaney insisted. "She's an amazing singer and tap dancer."

"Great." Kylie groaned. "Just what we need for a baking club. She can serenade us with show tunes while we mix ingredients."

"I do," Delaney said. "Remember last week? I did the entire score of *Hamilton* while we made patriotic pistachio cupcakes."

"I remember…"

"I thought my choice for a new PLC member should bring the same energy and enthusiasm to PLC that I do," Delaney insisted. "Besides, she's not exactly Miss Popularity at my school. Kids don't like that she says whatever she's thinking."

"Ew!" Whitney suddenly interjected. She had found Kylie's recipe notebook and started flipping through it. "It says we're baking raspberry cupcakes today. I hate raspberries. Those little seeds get in my teeth."

"Me too!" Delaney exclaimed. "And then you're trying to pick them out with your tongue in the middle of a song, and it's *so* annoying!"

"Well, she *is* just like you," Kylie said, teasing Delaney.

Lexi came in the room next, dragging a boy behind her by the hand. "Come on, Nathaniel," she urged him, yanking him through the door. "You can do it."

The kid's cheeks were bright red with embarrassment. "Lemme go!" He pleaded with Lexi. "I hate crowds."

"But there are only four of us in here," Kylie told him.

"That's four too many!" Nathaniel replied.

"He's shy," Lexi told her clubmates.

"No kidding." Delaney giggled. "I never would have guessed."

"Oh, do you have stage fright?" Whitney asked him. "I can help you with that. Just look around the room, and picture everyone here in pink polka-dot clown suits with red noses."

"You see? They think I'm a clown!" Clementine complained. She had just walked through the door with Sadie by her side.

"No one thinks you're a clown," Sadie insisted.

"I was telling him to think of all of us as clowns," Whitney explained. "You don't have to be one if you don't want to."

Sadie looked confused. "What's going on?"

Kylie shook her head. "I have no idea."

"We're not late, are we?" Jenna asked, bounding into the room breathlessly.

"Who's we?" Delaney asked her.

"*Ay, dios mío!*" Jenna exclaimed. "I swear, she was right behind me a minute ago!"

She peered outside the teachers' lounge and spied Roxy putting quarters in a vending machine.

"Roxy! There's no time for that!" Jenna called to her.

A pack of chips fell out of the machine. "There's always time for a snack!" Roxy insisted. "Sour cream and onion flavor!" She opened the pack and offered one to Jenna.

"Fine," Jenna said, popping a chip in her mouth. "Just get in there."

"Okay," Kylie said, taking a head count. "We have five original members and four junior members present."

"Where's your mini-me?" Sadie asked her.

Kylie hadn't given that much thought. "I was so busy putting up flyers that I guess I forgot to find one."

The door suddenly creaked open. "Is this the cupcake club meeting?" asked a tiny girl with a brown bob and glasses.

"Yes, it is," Lexi replied. "Are you here to join?"

"Well, maybe… I dunno. I saw your flyer," the girl answered. "I'm only in first grade, but I'm a really good baker. My mom says so."

"Wait! I know you!" Kylie suddenly remembered the first time she had posted a sign-up sheet for PLC a year ago. A kindergartner had come up to her, asking for the sticker on it—but she couldn't read what the sheet said. "Do you know how to read now?" Kylie asked her.

"Oh yes!" the girl said. "I'm seven, and I read recipes all the time." She picked a cookbook up off the table and turned to a random page. "'Sift the flour, baking soda, salt, and sugar in a large bowl. Combine the dry ingredients with the wet, being careful not to overmix…'"

"Impressive," Sadie said.

Delaney agreed. "'Though she be but little, she is fierce.'"

"What's that supposed to mean?" Roxy asked.

"It's a quote from Shakespeare," Whitney informed them. "*A Midsummer Night's Dream*. I did it in my theater camp."

"It means I think we have our junior club," Kylie said. "Your name is Brynn, right?"

The first grader beamed. "You remembered!"

"Do you think you could read this recipe so we can all follow it?" she asked, handing Brynn her binder.

"Raspberry Cupcakes with Vanilla Buttercream Frosting," Brynn read out loud.

"No nuts, right?" Clementine asked.

"Positively no nuts. PLC Jr. is a nut-free zone," Kylie assured her.

With each of the older girls guiding them, Brynn, Roxy, Whitney, Nathaniel, and Clementine assembled the ingredients, put them into the mixer, poured the batter into the muffin pans, and placed the cupcakes in the oven to bake. When the Junior PLCers took out the muffin pans twenty minutes later, the tops of the cakes were a delicate golden-brown color.

"Insert a toothpick in the center, and make sure it comes out clean," Sadie told Clementine.

The younger girl followed her directions. "Yup. It's clean," she said.

"Now you let them cool for fifteen minutes, or your frosting will melt right off," Delaney explained.

"And it gives us the perfect opportunity to discuss how we should decorate them," Kylie added.

"Nathaniel is a really talented artist," Lexi insisted. She held up a notebook that he had covered in doodles.

"Okay, Nate," Kylie said. "What should we draw on our cupcakes?"

Lexi handed him a piping bag and a paper plate. "Show them what you can do," she said, urging him on.

The boy took the bag and began creating an intricate swirl of pink frosting.

"Whoa," Sadie said. "He handles that bag like a pro."

"Can you make a rose?" Whitney asked him. "I love roses when I take my bows."

"Um, I guess," Nathaniel answered.

Lexi handed him a cooled cupcake, and the boy obliged, creating perfect pink petals.

Kylie could hardly believe her eyes—but the proof was in the cupcake. She handed one to Jenna to taste. "How'd they do?" she asked.

Jenna held the cupcake under her nose, took a sniff, then a lick of the frosting. "Sweet, delicate, a hint of Tahitian vanilla…" She took a tiny bite. "Nice berry flavor…not overpowering, but not wimpy either."

Roxy grabbed another cupcake off the cooling rack. "I think it could use a better balance of flavor between the frosting and the cake," she said thoughtfully. "Actually, I'd go with a dark chocolate buttercream instead of a vanilla frosting. That would bring out the raspberry flavor even more."

"Good point," Jenna admitted. "But ganache, not buttercream."

"And there are no seeds," Whitney said approvingly. "That trick of straining the puree really worked." She took a big bite. "Yum!"

Sadie turned to Clementine. "Anything you'd like to add?"

"I think we could bake more if we worked faster. Cracking one egg at a time is really slow."

Sadie handed her a bowl and a dozen eggs. "Okay, show us your stuff."

Clementine grabbed two eggs in each hand, tapped them simultaneously on the edge of the bowl, and flawlessly emptied their contents.

"Not a single shell," Sadie marveled, holding up the bowl. "Like I said, girl's got skills!"

Brynn surveyed the counter, tables, and stove top, all covered in flour, berry juice, and frosting. "It's really messy in here. We should probably clean up." The other junior members all groaned.

"None of that!" Delaney scolded them. "Cleanup can be just as much fun as making the mess."

"Do you remember our first bake?" Lexi recalled, chuckling. "When Kylie sat in a puddle of batter?"

"The Batter Butt Dance!" Kylie exclaimed. "How could I forget? We made up that crazy rap."

"Wait," Whitney interrupted her. "If anyone is going to sing and dance, you'd better leave it to the professionals. I danced onstage at a Bieber concert."

She stood on a chair, placing her hands on her hips, and turned to Roxy. "Give me a beat."

Roxy obliged, drumming with two wooden spoons on the back of a muffin tin. Whitney clapped along and began to rap: "Make it, cake it, go ahead and bake it! Who's the coolest club around? PLC! Can you take it?" She jumped down and took a bow.

"Yaaas!" Delaney applauded wildly. "That's awesome."

There was a knock on the door, and Herbie peeked in. "My robotics club meeting just let out. I wanted to see how you were all doing."

Kylie looked around the room. Club members old and new were laughing and mopping up the floors and table-tops together. "Not bad, not bad at all," she admitted.

The Write Stuff

Kylie had been so busy teaching her new junior cupcake club how to bake that she'd almost forgotten about the assignment Principal Fontina had given the entire fifth grade: a five-hundred-word essay on "What Blakely means to me." And it was due tomorrow! She was sitting at her desk, chewing on a pencil eraser, when Sadie called.

"I'm stumped," she said. "I have no idea what to write. I mean, I can think of a million things I wanna say, but it all comes out like a mishmash."

"Tell me," Kylie said, coaching her. "What does Blakely mean to you?"

"Well," Sadie began. "It means victory…like when we won the state basketball championship. And it also means defeat, like when I came in a close second in the citywide track meet but lost by just one second. But I wasn't a sore loser. I congratulated the girl who beat me."

"So it means sports?"

"No, not just sports. It also means learning to be a team on and off the court. It means friends who have your back no matter what. It means people who cheer you on, like Coach Walsh and you, Lexi, Jenna, and Delaney…"

"I think you have your essay," Kylie reassured her. "Now just put it down on paper."

Sadie thanked her and hung up—just as Lexi FaceTimed her.

"Okay, how does this sound?" she asked Kylie as her face appeared on the phone screen. "Blakely is my second home. I can't bear the thought of not walking through those red doors every morning…" She sniffled and blew her nose in a tissue. "It makes me so sad to think Blakely will soon be behind me, that this chapter of my life is coming to an end!"

"It's very moving," Kylie replied.

"You think it's too sappy," Lexi said. "I can see it on your face."

"How can you see anything when you're sobbing like that?" Kylie asked.

"Fine," Lexi said, wiping away her tears. "I'll throw in how much fun I had. That will brighten it up, don't you think?"

Kylie nodded. "Oh yeah. Tons."

"So what are you writing?" Lexi asked her.

"I have no idea," Kylie admitted. "It's like I put my pencil to the paper, and nothing comes out."

"Why?" Lexi asked.

"I wish I knew."

"Look at some old photos. Maybe they'll jog your memory and inspire you."

Kylie nodded. "Maybe. It's like my brain has Blakely block or something."

"Good luck!" Lexi said, hitting the print button on her laptop. "You'll come up with something. You always do."

Kylie flipped through photos on her phone. There was one of the Eco Fair, when PLC had baked "eco-licous" cupcakes; another of the girls delivering their first order to the Golden Spoon gourmet shop in Greenwich; and yet another of the floating cupcake display they'd made for a fashion show on a cruise ship. They'd created so many amazing recipes together…everything from cannoli cupcakes and dog-friendly pupcakes to banana peanut-butter fudge cupcakes that an Elvis impersonator in Vegas loved. Kylie's PLC binder housed a collection of their greatest recipes—all tried and tested and perfected with hard work, friendship, and laughter.

Her phone suddenly dinged with a text message from Jenna: Help me! I've got 1,600 words, and I can't delete any of them!

Kylie smiled and typed back, Edit. Then she picked up her pencil and began to write. When she looked up at the clock on her desk, thirty minutes had passed, and there was indeed something on her paper. She read it over once, then tucked it into her school binder. It might not have been what Principal Fontina asked for, but it was the truth. It would have to do.

It took over a week for Principal Fontina to announce the two winners of the essay contest over the school loudspeaker. "After much deliberation, the graduation committee has chosen two students to deliver commencement addresses." She read the first name: "Congratulations, Meredith Mitchell." No surprise there. Meredith had probably hired a famous political speechwriter to craft the best essay on the planet! But the next name took Kylie totally by surprise: "And our other speaker will be Kylie Carson. Great job, Kylie!"

"I thought you had Blakely block," Lexi said,

hugging her friend when they passed each other in the hall. "Congrats!"

"I can't believe it," Kylie replied. "I mean, all I wrote was a recipe."

Lexi looked baffled. "A recipe? You were supposed to write an essay."

"I know, but every time I thought of Blakely, I thought of our cupcake club and one of our recipes."

The second-period bell rang. "I'm sure it's great!" Lexi called as she raced to her art class. "Can't wait to hear it!"

Tomorrow was Assembly Day—and the first opportunity the speakers would have to practice their speeches. Kylie wasn't sure how she felt about sharing with the entire fifth grade. What she had written wasn't an essay. What if they laughed? What if they thought she was weird? What if she made a fool of herself on one of the most important days of her elementary school career? She found herself walking down the hall to the principal's office.

"I loved what you wrote," Principal Fontina said, noticing Kylie hovering outside her door.

"Um, that's what I was actually coming to talk to you about," Kylie said. "I changed my mind. I think someone else should deliver a commencement address, not me."

"Really? I'm surprised to hear that," Principal Fontina said. "Your speech was thoughtful and original. The committee voted unanimously to have you read it."

"Thanks, but no thanks," Kylie said. "I hope you understand."

"I don't," Principal Fontina replied. "And I'll hope you'll reconsider. At least promise me you'll think about it."

Kylie sighed. "Okay, but I don't think I'll change my mind."

A Cupcake Catastrophe

The next morning, Kylie heard her alarm go off and pulled the covers over her head. Her mom had to bribe her with her favorite chocolate-chip waffles just to get her to come downstairs. It felt like her fourth-grade monster movie presentation all over again! The thought of going to school—and practicing her silly recipe speech in front of an audience—made her queasy.

"I'm not feeling so good," she told her mom, who instantly felt her head.

"Cool as a cucumber, Kylie Carson," she replied. "You're fine."

"I'm not. I don't want to go to assembly today."

"I thought you said you loved assembly," her dad said when she appeared at the breakfast table. "What happened to all the excitement over graduating?"

"I'm excited about graduating…just not the graduation ceremony," Kylie explained.

"Why the change of heart?" her mom asked. "A week ago you couldn't wait to get to school."

"That was before I had to humiliate myself by speaking in front of the entire graduating class!" Kylie groaned.

Her mom stopped pouring syrup on her waffles. "What? That's great! You were chosen to make a speech?"

"It's not a speech. It's a recipe."

"Well, you're great at recipes," her dad pointed out. "I have never known you to make a cupcake that wasn't delicious."

"Well, this isn't a recipe for a cupcake. It's kind of a recipe for my years at Blakely."

"Sounds interesting," her mom assured her. "Like a metaphor."

"A really embarrassing metaphor that no one will get," Kylie said. "I don't know why I even turned it in. I just had to write something. I never thought they'd pick it."

"Give yourself some credit, Kylie," her dad said. "You've come a long way since you were the new kid. Your class-mates look up to you. You've done amazing things."

"I'm sure it will be very inspirational," her mom added.

"I told Principal Fontina I didn't want to read it."

Her dad frowned. "Since when is Smiley Kylie a quitter?" he asked. "So your essay is different. So it's unique. I say that's a winning formula right there."

Kylie tried to tell herself it would be okay, that Meredith wouldn't make fun of her and the entire fifth grade wouldn't burst into hysterical laughter. But all she could envision was the worst-case scenario: utter and complete humiliation.

When she got to the auditorium, Herbie was setting up the audio equipment and pushing a small podium to the front of the stage.

"Testing, one-two-three," he said into the microphone.

"Oh no… They're not going to make me read it over a mic, are they?" Kylie asked Jenna.

"Well, you want the folks in the very last row to hear it, don't you?"

"No, not really," Kylie said, sinking into her seat. Maybe if she closed her eyes, all this would just disappear.

"So, you're the other speaker." She opened one eye to find Meredith looming over her. "I'll go first. We don't want to bore the audience right away. At least let them have a little fun before you go on and kill the mood."

"Just remember it's a graduation speech, not an Oscar acceptance speech," Jenna taunted her. "No thanking Mumsy and Dadsie and your hair and makeup army."

Meredith narrowed her eyes. "Jealous much, Jenna?"

"Nope, not at all," Jenna tossed back. "To be jealous, I'd have to want something you have. And you've got nada."

Kylie appreciated her friend jumping to her defense, but none of this was helping the situation. She still had to get up there and read her weird recipe in front of dozens of fifth graders.

Herbie was anxiously checking his watch because the graduation coordinator Principal Fontina had hired was late. Kylie hoped he or she wouldn't show up at all and the assembly would be canceled. But just then, the door to the auditorium flung open and someone ran in, apologizing profusely.

"Sorry! Sorry! My flight was delayed, and then I couldn't get a cab from the airport…" Kylie's stomach did a flip-flop. She knew that voice!

"So, who's ready to put on a great graduation show?" Juliette climbed the steps to the stage, hugged her brother, Herbie, and waved to the students in the audience.

"You all remember my sister, Juliette Dubois… I mean Higgins," Herbie said. "She's a married lady now."

"Hello, all!" Juliette said, grinning. "It's so good to be back at Blakely!"

"Juliette is here? How? Why?" Kylie gasped. She rubbed her eyes to make sure her old cupcake club adviser wasn't a figment of her imagination.

"I thought she was living in London with Rodney!" Jenna whispered. "Wow, she knows how to make an entrance."

"My husband is directing a new play on Broadway, which means I get to be here with all of you till graduation," Juliette explained.

Kylie couldn't believe it. This was the best news she'd had all week!

"So let me have my two speakers up here to start things off…Meredith and Kylie."

Meredith practically ran up to the stage, but Jenna had to give Kylie a push.

"Who wants to go first, ladies?" Juliette asked them.

"Me!" Meredith volunteered and seized the mic out of Juliette's hand.

"Good! That'll give us some time for a proper catch-up,"

Juliette said, pulling Kylie to the wings of the stage and hugging her. "I've missed you guys so much!"

"And we've missed you," Kylie told her. "But Herbie's done a really good job filling in."

"I'm sure he has," Juliette replied. "I trained him well."

"Oh! Speaking of training, we've got a junior cupcake club now that we're teaching how to bake," Kylie told her.

"Yes, it was my suggestion to Principal Fontina. I don't think Blakely should ever be without a cupcake club. That's your gift to this school, Kylie."

"Oh," Kylie said, surprised. "I wasn't into it at first, but now I think these kids are pretty great. And they're learning so fast."

"Just like all of you did," Juliette reminded her. "It took time, but you got to be experts. Now it's your turn to pass that knowledge on."

Kylie glanced out at the stage. Meredith was still droning on, something about how she was "a shining example of the power of youth to change the world."

"I'm looking forward to your speech," Juliette told her.

"Oh, about that…"

"I heard it's different. Very creative and one of a kind. Not unlike the girl who wrote it."

Kylie gulped. "Can someone else give a speech instead? I'm sure Sadie wouldn't mind. Hers is really strong. Or Lexi, although she'll probably need a box of tissues to get through it."

"You really don't want to read yours? I won't force you," Juliette said.

Kylie shook her head.

"Okay, then we'll move on." She walked over to Meredith and cut her off. "Your speech should be no more than three minutes long," Juliette reminded her. "You'll have to edit it down."

"Three minutes?" Meredith moaned. "But it's over six minutes without the poem and my lyrical dance solo!"

Kylie climbed off the stage and walked quietly back to her seat.

"*Qué pasó, chica?*" Jenna whispered.

"Nothing. I just don't need to stand up and give a speech."

Kylie felt tapping on her shoulder. "But you do need to help us." Brynn had snuck into the auditorium and had been searching high and low for Kylie.

"Why? What happened?" Kylie asked, concerned.

"It's a cupcake catastrophe," Brynn told her. "Come quick!"

When they reached the Blakely teachers' lounge, Kylie smelled something burning.

"Why are you guys even in here?" she asked Brynn. "You're newbies! You're not supposed to use the kitchen unsupervised and not unless we have a meeting after school."

"I know. I know," Brynn apologized. "But we had this recipe we needed to test out. It was supposed to be a surprise. We wanted to show you we could do it all by ourselves like big kids."

She opened the door, and smoke poured out of the room. Clementine was on a stool, fanning the smoke detector so it wouldn't go off.

"We messed up," Nathaniel told her. "Big-time."

"Define *messed up*," Kylie said, surveying the damage. There were large puddles of water on the floor and batter splashes everywhere—even on the window curtains.

"We didn't think it would burn, but then it did, so we got the extinguisher…" Brynn tried to explain as best she could. All Kylie could see was white foam covering the couch.

"You set the teachers' lounge on fire?" Kylie gasped.

"I wouldn't call it a fire…more like a few sparks,"

Nathaniel said, staring down at his shoes. "I took the cup-cakes out of the oven, and the flames scared me, so I kind of threw the muffin tin…"

"And it landed on the couch," Clementine continued. "And the fabric got a little toasty." She held up a singed pillow.

"It's my fault. The recipe called for twenty minutes in the oven, and I forgot to set the timer," Brynn apologized.

"And I distracted her into watching this funny video on YouTube so the cupcakes baked for over an hour," Clementine said.

"But I threw the tin," Nathaniel said. "I made it worse!"

Kylie sat down on a sticky stool and tried to think. "Okay, all the teachers are still at assembly, so we have about fifteen minutes to get rid of the evidence." The room smelled like burned cupcakes. "Open the windows wide," she instructed the kids. "And get a roll of paper towels to wipe up the water and the rest of this mess."

"What about the toasty pillow?" Brynn asked her.

"Hide it," Kylie said, opening a cupboard door beneath the sink. "No one will ever look here." She fluffed the rest of the pillows and tossed a fringed throw over the back of the couch so no one would notice the stain. "It'll have to do for now," Kylie told them. "But you're going to have to tell Principal Fontina eventually…and pay for the damage."

"Pay?" Brynn's eyes grew big. "I don't have enough money in my piggy bank to buy a new teachers' lounge!"

"I don't think you'll have to buy a whole new lounge—just maybe a few pillows and have the curtains dry-cleaned," Kylie explained. "Still, you'll have to earn the money to pay the school back."

"Earn it? How?" Brynn asked.

"By helping us tomorrow on a big cupcake order. You guys thought you were ready to be in business. Well, here's your chance to prove it."

6

Big-Top Bake

Mrs. Carson did a double take as she watched all the members of PLC Jr. file into her kitchen.

"Kylie," she inquired. "Who are all these kids? Did you call in the cavalry?"

"Kind of… They're helping," she explained.

"They're bakers in training," Delaney added. She pulled Whitney over. "This one's my mini-me. It's like if I were Britney Spears, she'd be my backup dancer."

"Oh, no I'm not," Whitney protested. "I'm no one's backup dancer. I'm a star." She pulled away from Delaney and went back to helping the others unpack the ingredients.

"Your mini-me has a mighty mouth." Jenna chuckled. "She certainly told you off."

"Well, yours is eating all the ingredients before we can get them into the cupcakes," Delaney pointed out. Roxy had found a bag of mini M&M's and was helping herself to several handfuls.

"Drop those candies!" Jenna bellowed. "There is no tasting unless I say so."

Roxy swallowed what was already in her mouth. "Well, you can't expect us to work without feeding us," she said. "That's cruel and unusual punishment."

"You set the Blakely teachers' lounge on fire," Kylie reminded them. "This *is* your punishment. Be grateful we talked to Principal Fontina, and she's letting you pay for the damages."

"Was she mad?" Nathaniel whispered. "Like red-in-the-face, steam-coming-out-of-her-ears furious?"

Kylie shook her head. "Well, she was at first. Then I reminded her that she had asked us to start this junior cupcake club."

"Exactly!" Jenna said. "We would never overbake our cupcakes or set things on fire."

"But we did—a lot—when we first started out," Lexi reminded her. "We were total disasters."

"Remember when we made a cupcake ball gown and rolled me into a birthday party...and I fell flat on my face?" Delaney recalled. "I thought that carpet would be ruined forever with frosting stains."

"How about the time our giant cupcake wedding cake melted in the heat?" Sadie recalled. "What a wreck that was!"

"Or the time we made a cupcake pirate ship, and it sank?" Jenna added.

"Sounds like you guys messed up just as much as we did," Brynn said, overhearing. "Maybe even more. So, like my mommy says, you need to forgive and forget."

Kylie stared. This tiny first grader was certainly protective of her newfound clubmates. "You think so, huh?"

"Yup," Brynn insisted. "We know now that you have to set the timer when you start the oven."

"For sure," Sadie told her. "Baking is an exact science. If the recipe says twenty minutes, you check it in twenty minutes."

Brynn placed an egg timer on the kitchen counter. "I even borrowed one of these from Mommy to make sure."

Kylie smiled. "That's good thinking, Brynn. And very responsible of you."

"You sure she's only seven years old?" Delaney asked Kylie. "She sounds kinda bossy and authoritative."

"She sounds like *you*," Jenna said to Kylie. "She's your mini-me!"

Kylie watched as Brynn circled around the kitchen,

making sure everything was assembled where it should be, the oven was preheated, and the mixer was plugged in and ready to go. "Did you all wash your hands?" she asked her team. "Clean hands in the kitchen!"

"My mom says I need to be home in two hours to study for my social studies test," Nathaniel told her.

Brynn scowled. "That will never be enough time to bake and decorate eight dozen cupcakes for this order!" She held up a form that read "Dylan's Fifth Birthday Circus Party."

"Do the math," Sadie instructed Nathaniel. "How many cupcakes are in eight dozen?"

Nathaniel wrinkled his brow and did some calculating on his fingers. "Eight times twelve… That's ninety-six."

"Yes! Give the kid a gold star!" Jenna applauded.

"We don't have any gold stars," Roxy pointed out. "But we have some mini marshmallows."

"Then give the kid a mini marshmallow," Jenna said after reconsidering. "Now you. How many cupcakes can we make in the oven at once?"

Roxy walked over, opened the oven door, and peered inside. "Let's see. So twelve cupcakes go in one tin, and I'd say four muffin tins will fit in there—so that's four times twelve, or forty-eight cupcakes at once."

"Ding-ding-ding!" Delaney sang. "A mini marshmallow for you!"

"One!" Jenna reminded Roxy, grabbing the bag before she could take a handful.

Kylie looked at Brynn. "So how long will it take to bake that batch of four dozen cupcakes?"

Brynn didn't hesitate. "Eighteen to twenty-two minutes, depending on the heat of the oven."

"And how long to decorate?" Lexi asked Nathaniel.

"Well, fifteen minutes to cool the cupcake, then about two minutes to frost each one."

"But what if we're adding polka dots and rainbow swirls to each one? And what if we're assembling them on a big-top stage that's covered in candy?"

Nathaniel sighed. "We have to build the stage and paint it, and then mix multicolored frosting to swirl on the cupcakes. I'm never gonna be home by six."

"Ooh! I can help build the big top," Clementine insisted. "Circuses are kind of my thing."

"If we quickly mix the batter, I think we can bake eight dozen in about an hour," Brynn said. "Which leaves us another whole hour to make it look circusy."

"Is *circusy* a word?" Sadie whispered to Kylie.

"I'm not sure, but I don't think it matters. They totally get what to do!"

She turned to face the mini bakers. "All right, you guys, the clock's ticking. Who's got the recipe?"

Brynn held up the club binder. "Confetti cupcakes with rainbow swirl buttercream."

"Sounds pretty," Lexi said. "And a little complicated. You sure you're ready for this?"

Brynn put down the binder and clapped her hands together. "PLC Jr.," she commanded. "Let's show 'em what we can do."

While the juniors worked diligently on baking the cupcakes, Sadie laid a large, round piece of plywood from her dad's contracting company on the kitchen table. Her dad had built a dome-shaped cover over it that was supported by wooden dowels in its center and on the sides. "Ta-da! Your big top," she said.

"How are we going to drape the sides of the circus tent?" Delaney asked.

"I'm thinking red and yellow fondant stripes," Lexi said. "With a bright-blue flag up top and mini marshmallows and candy decorating the circus rings."

"I'll color and roll out the fondant," Delaney volunteered.

"And I'll make the flag and maybe some cute little animals and a ringmaster out of modeling chocolate," Lexi added. She waved at Nathaniel, who was frantically frosting cupcakes. "Hand that piping bag to Clementine," she instructed him. "Let's see your sculpting skills."

Within minutes, the boy had managed to make a miniature elephant and lion.

"Whoa, he's good," Jenna observed. "As good as you, Lexi."

Lexi didn't like the sound of that. "Well, the ears on the elephant could be bigger," she said, flattening them out with a tool. "But they're okay."

Each of the PLC girls went around the room, instructing their students. "Tap the shell quickly and crisply," Sadie told Clementine. "It's all in the wrist. And you can do two eggs in each hand."

Clementine nodded. "Eggs are smaller than the balls I juggle. I might be able to do three in one hand, but that would be showing off."

Jenna taught Roxy how to differentiate between Tahitian and Madagascar vanilla. "You see how the Madagascar is uncomplicated and straightforward," she said, placing a dot on the tip of Roxy's tongue. "Now taste the Tahitian."

Roxy closed her eyes and licked her lips. "There's just a tiny hint of sweet fruitiness to it," she said.

"*Eso es increíble,*" Jenna said. "You have really fine-tuned taste buds."

Delaney demonstrated for Whitney how to use an ice cream scoop to fill each cupcake liner precisely. "It has to be two-thirds full. If you pour too much, your cupcakes blob over the sides," she said.

"And if you pour too little, you wind up with flat, sad ones," Whitney said. "When it comes to accessories and cupcake batter, less isn't always more."

Brynn circled the room, jotting things down in a notebook and trying to take it all in. "I know it's a lot to learn," Kylie said, sitting down on a stool. "It took me forever, but now I could probably bake cupcakes with my eyes closed."

"Oh no," Brynn insisted, flipping back to the first page where she had written down Sadie's directive. "Baking is a science. If you close your eyes, you can't see what's in the measuring cup. And that could mess up everything."

"You're right," Kylie said. "I stand corrected."

"But you're sitting," Brynn pointed out.

Oh my, Kylie thought. *This munchkin takes things so seriously!*

"It's a figure of speech," Kylie tried to explain.

"Oh, like the speech you're making at graduation."

Kylie's face turned pale. "No, I'm not making any speech."

"That's not what I heard," Brynn said. "I heard Principal Fontina telling Herbie it was the best graduation speech she'd ever read."

"She said that?" Kylie gasped.

"Uh-huh," Brynn insisted. "Can I hear it?"

"What?"

"The speech," Brynn pressed.

"It's not a speech. It's just something silly I wrote down."

Brynn flipped to a page tucked into the back of the recipe binder. "Is this it? 'The Recipe for Success'?"

Kylie grabbed the paper out of Brynn's hands. "You weren't supposed to see that!" she exclaimed.

"Well, you asked me to open to the recipe page, and it was just sitting right there in your book," Brynn said. "I think it's really good. I mean, I haven't read a lot of things in first grade, but I definitely think it's better than 'Twinkle, Twinkle, Little Star.'"

Kylie tucked the paper in the back pocket of her jeans.

"Thanks," she said. "'Twinkle, Twinkle' is a tough act to follow."

Brynn shrugged. "Do you think we made enough money today to buy the teachers new pillows and clean the curtains?"

"I think we've got it covered," Kylie assured her. "And I'm sure Principal Fontina will be willing to forgive and forget…if you save her one of these." She held up a perfectly frosted rainbow-swirl cupcake.

"I made extra," Brynn said. "In case a few got messed up."

"That's smart thinking," Kylie said. "I always make an extra one or two dozen in case of a cupcake emergency."

"I know. I saw it in your speech…I mean, the thing I wasn't supposed to see. It was under the ingredients: 'Be prepared. Always have extras on hand for an emergency.'"

"You remembered that?" Kylie asked.

"Yup. Mommy says I have a photogenic memory."

"A photo*graphic* memory!" Kylie giggled. "It means you remember whatever you read. That's an amazing ability."

Brynn seemed more concerned with the extra cupcakes. "So what do we do with them now?"

Kylie smiled brightly and handed her the platter to pass around. "We eat them!"

7

A Sticky Situation

Kylie knew that an integral part of the cupcake club wasn't just baking and decorating the cupcakes—it was getting them to the client on time and in one piece. So if her junior club was *really* going to eat, sleep, and breathe cupcakes, they had to understand the process from start to finish. For that reason, she invited Brynn, Nathaniel, Roxy, Whitney, and Clementine along to make the delivery. They were waiting at her house early on Saturday morning when Sadie's father drove up in his delivery van.

"Careful, careful, go slow," she instructed as the juniors all gathered around the big-top display and gently hoisted it off Kylie's kitchen table. Lexi had outdone herself with the decorations: a beautiful striped circus tent, three rings outlined in mini marshmallows, and a floor made of toasted, shredded coconut "hay." The cupcakes sat in each ring, stacked on risers, amid tiny acrobats, clowns, and animals made out of modeling chocolate.

"I can't look," Sadie said, covering her eyes, as the youngsters carried the display through the living room toward the front door.

"Brynn, hold it higher on your side," Kylie said. "Don't tilt, or things will fall off." She spoke too soon. A cupcake landed with a *kerplop* on the front doorstep.

"Oh, no!" Brynn cried. "I ruined it!"

"It's okay," Kylie assured her. "You made extras, remember?"

"I'm losing my grip!" Nathaniel suddenly yelped as his side of the display swayed.

"Steady! Steady!" Sadie shouted. "Put your back into it. Use some muscle!"

"What muscle?" Nathaniel whined. "I don't have any."

"OMG, I think I broke a nail!" Whitney said, letting go of the wood base to examine her manicure.

"Never let go!" Kylie commanded, quickly stepping in to support the open spot. "You're a team. You have to work together. All hands in."

Whitney complained but took hold of her side of the display. Little by little, they inched their way out to Mr. Harris's minivan.

"Where does it go?" Roxy asked.

"Only place it will fit…the back of the van," Sadie's father explained. "I folded down some of the seats so you can slide it right in. Some of you can sit in the middle and two of you in the back."

"I get carsick in the back of vans," Whitney insisted.

"And when did you ever ride in the back of a van?" Roxy asked her.

"Well, never. But I don't want to risk it."

Kylie rolled her eyes and was about to reprimand them when Roxy spoke up. "Brynn and I will take the back seats."

"Don't worry. I'll drive real slow," Mr. Harris assured them.

They eased the big top into the back and climbed in. "Keep a close eye on things," Kylie told Brynn. "It's a good thirty-minute drive to the party, and a lot can happen to cupcakes in thirty minutes."

While the others chattered away, Brynn sat staring at the cupcake display. She held her breath every time Mr. Harris stopped short or sped around a curve.

"How's it going back there?" Sadie glanced over her shoulder.

"Nathaniel is drawing a portrait of me in his sketchbook," Whitney said, batting her eyelashes.

"Make sure you make her head *really* big," Clementine teased. "If you want it to be true to life."

Roxy was too busy chewing gum and staring out the window to pay attention to their discussion. She blew a huge bubble and let it pop.

"Whoa!" Clementine noticed the size. "That could be a world-record bubble."

"How many pieces does it take to make one that big?" Nathaniel asked, curious.

Roxy examined her pack of grape Bubble Yum. "Well, there's ten pieces to a pack…and I only have five left."

"Gimme!" Whitney said, reaching back to snatch a piece out of her hand. "I challenge you to a bubble blow-off."

"Yes!" Roxy cheered. "You're on! Get this on your phone," she instructed Nathaniel.

Whitney's bubble-blowing skills were impressive, but Roxy was not going to be outdone. She popped yet another piece of gum in her mouth. It was almost too much to chew!

Just then, the van came to an abrupt halt in traffic—and the giant wad of gum flew out of her mouth and landed right on the big top!

"Oh my gosh! Oh my gosh!" Brynn cried in panic. As

she tried to pull the gum off, pieces of the fondant tore away—and the purple dye stained the yellow stripes a weird shade of gray. The gum hung in a sticky, stringy mess from the top of the tent.

"Don't touch it!" Nathaniel pleaded with her. "You're making it worse."

"It can't be any worse," Brynn shot back. "The big top is destroyed!"

"What's going on back there?" Kylie called, hearing a commotion.

"Oh, nothing," Roxy said. "Nathaniel just burped."

"Did not!"

"Did too!" Roxy shouted. "You know how boys are!"

"I've got two brothers… I do," Sadie said, chuckling.

"We have to do something—fast!" Brynn whispered to her junior crew.

"There's traffic up ahead. We're going to be sitting here for quite a while," Mr. Harris warned his passengers.

"Oh, thank goodness," Brynn said, mopping her brow. "Nate, can you climb back here while we're standing still in traffic and fix it?"

"After you just humiliated me by saying I burped in public?"

Brynn looked him in the eye. "We need you to fix this," she said sternly. "Before Kylie and Sadie see and we get kicked out of the cupcake club for good."

"Fine," Nate replied, gathering the spare bag of fondant and frosting Kylie had packed "in case of emergencies" and climbing in the back. "I think I can maybe patch the mess with a fresh piece of fondant."

"What about this?" Clementine asked, holding up a circus elephant that had somehow fallen out of the display and rolled under the seats. His trunk was broken off.

"Where's the missing piece?" Nate asked, searching around frantically. "I can't sculpt a whole new figure from scratch. We have to find the trunk, and I can maybe reattach it."

Roxy, Whitney, and Clementine all began poking around under their seats. It was nowhere to be found.

"Let's do the repair on the tent first, then figure out what to do for Elinore," Nathaniel finally suggested.

"Who's Elinore?" Whitney asked.

"My elephant," Nathaniel replied.

"You named your chocolate elephant?" Roxy giggled. "Okay, that's not weird."

Nathaniel bit his lip. "Well, at least I didn't drool purple gum all over our display."

"I didn't drool," Roxy fired back. "I spit."

"Wait! I found Elinore's nose!" Whitney said, picking something up off the floor of the van. A small, brown squiggly object rested in the palm of her hand.

Brynn examined it carefully. "That's not chocolate. I think it's a worm."

"Eeeek!" Whitney screamed, dropping it.

Now Sadie and Kylie knew something was up.

"Guys, what's going on back there?" Kylie asked.

"Nothing! Nothing!" Brynn insisted. "Nathaniel burped again, and Whitney thinks it's gross."

"Would you stop?" Nathaniel begged her. "Stop blaming me for burping when I'm not! It's embarrassing!"

Clementine came to his rescue. "That wasn't Nate. That was me," she said, punctuating her sentence with a loud belch. "See?"

Sadie looked at Kylie. "Seriously? They're having a burping contest?"

Kylie shrugged. "Kids. What can I say?"

"And why are you in the back?" Sadie asked, noticing Nathaniel had switched seats.

"He gets sick in the middle row of vans," Whitney fibbed.

"But he's all buckled up again, safe and sound," Roxy assured them. "All good!"

Nathaniel smoothed the yellow fondant over the stained stripe and admired his handiwork. "I don't think it's very noticeable, do you?"

"It looks fine," Brynn said. "But what about Elinore?"

"I have a Tootsie Roll in my bag," Roxy volunteered. "I was saving it for later when I got hungry."

"When are you *not* hungry?" Whitney muttered.

"It'll have to do. Gimme," Nathaniel said, holding out his hand. He broke off a tiny piece and warmed it in the palms of his hands till it was malleable. He shaped it into a tiny, narrow log.

"How do we make it stick?" Brynn asked.

"I don't know. Fondant and frosting don't seem to wanna hold it," Nathaniel replied, frustrated.

"How about gum?" Roxy asked. "It's super sticky, right?"

She popped a piece in her mouth and chewed it before depositing it in Nathaniel's palm.

"Ew, you people are disgusting," Whitney said, wrinkling her nose.

Nathaniel broke off a tiny piece and placed it on the end of the Tootsie Roll trunk. Like magic, it stuck to Elinore's face.

And it was just in the nick of time. Mr. Harris was pulling the van into the venue parking lot.

"Quick!" Brynn whispered. "Put Elinore back inside the tent!"

Just then, Kylie opened the back of the truck and peered inside. "Did our big top survive the trip?"

"Don't you mean did *we* survive the trip?" Whitney asked. "Barely."

Brynn elbowed her in the ribs. "She means it's good. All good!"

Kylie raised an eyebrow and inspected the display. Everything looked perfect.

"Good job, PLC Jr.," she commended them. "See how easy that was?"

Brynn let out a huge sigh of relief. "Yeah, piece of cake."

The Kidz Zone Play Gym was decorated like a real circus with colored lights, balloons, banners, and a costumed clown with a big, red nose greeting guests.

"You must be Peace, Love, and Cupcakes," the clown said.

"And you must be a size fifteen!" Roxy said, noting his huge floppy shoes.

"I'm actually Dylan's dad, Mr. Latner. Shh! Don't tell."

"Your secret's safe with us," Kylie said. "Where would you like us to put the cupcake display?"

"Yeah, it's really heavy." Nathaniel huffed and puffed.

"Right in the middle of the gym on the large, round table," Mr. Latner instructed them.

"So where's the birthday boy?" Sadie asked, looking around the space. She saw several kids swinging from mini trapezes and a few jumping on a trampoline.

Kylie zoned in on a small child dressed like a ring-master in a red coat and black top hat. "I think I found him," she said.

After they gently placed the cupcakes on the table, Kylie took Brynn with her to meet Dylan.

"Happy birthday!" Kylie said. "We hope you like your cupcakes."

The boy's face suddenly turned bright red, and he let out a wail. "Cupcakes? I said I wanted an ice cream cake! Cupcakes are for babies!" He collapsed on the gym floor, kicking and screaming.

"Wow," Brynn said. "Does this happen a lot?"

"Um, not usually," Kylie replied, trying to soothe the screaming child. "Usually our clients love what we deliver."

Dylan's mother raced over to see why her son was in hysterics.

"He said he doesn't want cupcakes," Brynn said. "Which is silly. Because I'm a first grader, and I know that cupcakes are way better than ice cream cake."

Dylan stopped howling and sat up. "I'm going to kin-dergarten next year," he announced proudly, wiping away his tears.

"You are? Well, then you'll be able to tell everyone how

much you love cupcakes." Brynn smiled knowingly. "And they'll think you're a big kid."

"They will?" he asked.

"Absolutely," Kylie chimed in. "With the coolest birthday party ever."

His mother scooped him up and put the top hat back on his head. "Why don't you go jump on the trampoline?" she suggested. With that, the birthday boy was off and in a great mood again.

"Thanks," Mrs. Latner said. "If you hadn't told him what first graders think, I'm afraid that would have been a major meltdown."

Brynn smiled proudly. "Well, it's true. I had an ice cream cake shaped like a whale for my fifth birthday, and it was so frozen my mom couldn't even cut it. We all had to wait thirty minutes to have a piece, and then it tasted like freezer burn. Now, who wants that?"

"My thoughts precisely, which is why I hired you," Mrs. Latner said, handing a check to Kylie. "And a little tip for the delivery…and defusing Dylan's tantrum." She gave Brynn two twenty-dollar bills.

"Wow! Thanks!" Brynn exclaimed.

Kylie plucked the money out of her fingers. "For

dry-cleaning the curtains in the teachers' lounge," she reminded Brynn.

They turned to head for the door but stopped in their tracks, stunned by what was in front of them. There, surrounded by a crowd of applauding kids, was Clementine. She was juggling colorful beanbags and riding a unicycle!

"More! More!" the crowd chanted. So Roxy obliged and tossed her another…and another until she had six beanbags suspended in the air.

"She's a circus act!" Brynn said, amazed.

"She's a really *great* circus act," Kylie added.

"You didn't tell us the cupcakes came with entertainment," Mr. Latner said appreciatively.

"We didn't know," Brynn said, but Kylie quickly covered the first grader's mouth with her hand.

"She means we didn't know that you didn't know. Yes, Clementine is a wonderful performer… Well worth the extra fee, don't you think?"

"Extra fee? Of course! How much?"

"How much do you suppose two new throw pillows will cost?" Brynn asked.

"Forty dollars will be just fine," Kylie said, holding out her hand.

Mr. Latner looked over at Clementine who was now weaving in and out of the circle of children and juggling four large rubber balls in the air. Whitney was singing, "The wheel on the unicycle goes round and round," while Roxy and Nathaniel were tooting along on party horns.

"I'll make it sixty dollars—if they'll stay for another fifteen minutes so I can change out of this clown suit," Mr. Latner said. "It's really itchy!"

Kylie, Sadie, and PLC Jr. stayed much longer than that—until the party was over, and Dylan had devoured not one but three of his rainbow-swirl cupcakes.

Kylie handed the one hundred dollars in cash to Brynn. "This is for you to give Principal Fontina Monday morning," she said. "With a big apology and a promise that you will never set the lounge on fire again."

Brynn nodded. "Got it."

"Great job, juniors," Sadie added. "You should be proud of the work. You each brought something really special to the party today. Even if you did get purple gum all over the big-top tent."

Brynn's face fell. "You knew? How?"

"Small van, loud kids," Kylie said, laughing. "We wanted to see if you could figure it out for yourselves, and you did."

9

A Vote for Cupcakes

Kylie turned the page on the calendar to the next month and pinned it to the bulletin board in the teachers' lounge. It was already May 1, and graduation was only two weeks away!

"It snuck up on you, didn't it?" Herbie asked, noting that she looked worried.

"Kind of. I just don't know if they're ready."

"*They're* ready?" Herbie asked.

"PLC Jr.," she replied. "Filling an order for five hundred cupcakes is like running a marathon."

"Oh, and you're ready…to graduate, I mean."

Kylie thought for a moment. "Well, yeah. At least I thought I was. But now I have the juniors to think about. We have so much left to teach them."

"Well, you have two weeks to do it," Herbie said. "Just make sure those lessons stick so they can carry on when you leave. PLC has to mean to them what it means to all of you."

Kylie gulped. That was a huge responsibility! She could teach the club to mix and bake and pipe. But working together as a team and building an ironclad friendship that could weather any situation—good, bad, or messy—was a whole other story.

The door creaked open. Brynn was always the first to arrive for a cupcake club meeting. She liked to go over the binder with Kylie, noting every order—what was needed and when it was due—and carefully writing it down in her own composition notebook.

"Can we talk about the graduation cupcakes?" Brynn asked. She was already one step ahead of Kylie! "How long do you think it will take us to make them, and how much flour do you need for five hundred cupcakes? Oh, and how do you spell *graduation*?"

Kylie sat down and flipped to a recipe for chocolate–chocolate chip cupcakes. It was one of her favorites, one of the first that the club had perfected. "I think we'll do one hundred of these," she said. "But I'm open to suggestions for the other flavors."

Brynn dug in her backpack. "I was hoping you'd say that. I have some ideas." She pulled out several recipe books with bright-colored Post-its marking some of the pages. Before she could barrel ahead, Kylie stopped her. "So, everyone in the cupcake club has a say in what we do. Everyone gets a vote."

"Oh," Brynn said. "So we have to wait till everyone else gets here?"

"Exactly," Herbie said. "Which is why punctuality is so important."

"What's punkuality?" Brynn asked. "And where do you get it?"

"It means being on time," Kylie explained. "Which is something Herbie never is. Just be warned."

"I am today," he said, pointing to the clock. "I was bright and early because I know how important graduation is."

The rest of the club trickled in between three thirty-five and three forty-five. "Punkuality is important," Brynn told them. "The meeting is supposed to start at three thirty sharp."

"Who put the peanut in charge?" Jenna asked, laughing.

"Peanuts? I'm allergic to peanuts," Clementine said.

"We meant Brynn," Jenna assured her. "The only nut here is Delaney."

"Hey!" Delaney protested. "I prefer colorful or zany, thank you."

"I prefer we start the meeting," Herbie interrupted. "I have a robotics club waiting down the hall as well."

"Okay, let's brainstorm graduation cupcakes," Kylie began. "Flavors, frosting, decorations."

"Diplomas, caps," Lexi suggested.

"What if we make a giant graduation cap out of minis?" Sadie jumped in.

"Or a real diploma…with cupcakes all around it?" Delaney offered.

"What about a graduation gown covered in cupcakes?" Whitney said. "I volunteer to model it."

"Those are all good ideas," Kylie said, mulling it over. "But I feel like we could come up with something more original. We're PLC; we don't do the expected."

"Blakely," Nathaniel said softly.

"Yeah, we know our school name," Roxy said. "What about it?"

"What if we made Blakely out of mini cupcakes?"

The room fell silent, and everyone stared. Nathaniel's cheeks flushed, and he buried his head in his hands.

"No! Nathaniel, it's genius!" Kylie said. "Absolutely genius."

He looked up. "It is?"

Lexi took out her notebook and began to sketch. "We could make the school and the yard and the big, red doors in front."

"What will the cupcakes taste like?" Roxy asked.

Jenna high-fived her. "Good question. The flavors have to be just as original as the display."

"Oh! I have an idea!" Brynn said, flipping to a page in her notebook where she'd drawn a picture of a cupcake and placed a small cupcake sticker in the middle of it. "What if we bake a mini cupcake inside a regular one? A cupcake in a cupcake."

"So you take a bite and there's a whole other cupcake inside?" Kylie asked.

"Uh-huh," Brynn said. "Like chocolate inside vanilla, or vanilla inside chocolate."

"Or caramel inside German chocolate." Jenna continued Brynn's thought. "Or lemon–poppy seed inside piña colada. The possibilities are endless."

"It's kind of poetic if you think about it," Herbie said. "A junior cupcake and a regular cupcake combined…like you're doing with PLC."

Kylie closed her binder. "I say we have a game plan. All in favor, say 'Sprinkles.'"

Clementine raised her hand. "What do you mean 'in favor'? Like party favors?"

"Like you agree that this is a great idea," Delaney explained. "We all vote, and if we like the idea, we say 'Sprinkles.'"

"And what if we don't like the idea?" Whitney asked.

"Well, you say nothing," Sadie added. "And the majority wins, although we like it to be unanimous."

Brynn sighed. "I'm not sure what a youn-animal is, but I say 'Sprinkles' and vote yes."

"Anyone else?" Kylie asked.

The rest of the group shouted "Sprinkles!"—even Whitney.

"Now comes the fun part," Kylie said. "We get baking."

If at First You Don't Succeed

It took the cupcake club and its eager assistants three days to perfect their cupcake-in-a-cupcake recipe—with lots of mistakes in between.

"There is a burned cupcake inside here," Jenna said, taking a bite and spitting it out. "You can't overbake the minis. They bake much faster than the regular ones. This French vanilla tastes like it was barbecued!"

Lexi didn't like how placing the mini inside made the batter spill over the top of the wrapper. "It's just not pretty," she said.

Delaney giggled. "It looks like an overstuffed cupcake... a cupcake that ate too much!"

Kylie finally found the solution in a baking supply store: a muffin pan that held forty-eight mini cupcakes. "See? Teeny, tiny ones. They won't take up too much room inside the regular cupcakes."

"Do we frost them?" Sadie asked. "Or would that be weird to cover with raw batter when we bake?"

"I think it's fine to give them a tiny dot of icing." Kylie contemplated the idea. "As long as we freeze them first for about an hour—so they're hard and the icing doesn't get lost right away in the batter."

"Even if it does melt in, that's okay," Jenna added. "The flavor will still be there."

They tried the recipe again and again until it was perfect. And the new trays allowed them to bake 192 minis at one time!

Kylie sat down on a kitchen stool and began chewing on her pencil eraser.

"That means she's thinking really hard," Delaney whispered to the juniors.

"So how do we work these cupcakes into a Blakely school building display?" Kylie pondered out loud.

Now it was Lexi's turn to present some possible solutions. "I sketched it out. See the redbrick building with the gray roof and the green grass around it?"

"We can ask my dad to help us build a strong wooden base and a rectangular structure with doors and windows cut out," Sadie added. "Maybe we could even incorporate LED lights and a school bell."

"Fancy!" Clementine said. "I like it."

"Where do the cupcakes come into it?" Kylie asked.

Nathaniel raised his hand shyly. "We use red-velvet minis to cover the walls and green ones frosted with a grass piping tip for the lawn."

Kylie closed her eyes and tried to picture it. "I like it, but a display with that many cupcakes would be…"

"Ginormous?" Lexi interrupted her. "We'd have to actually build it on a rolling table."

"My dad can help us do that," Sadie said. "And don't forget the five hundred cupcakes to hand out. Where do those go?"

Lexi took out her colored pencils and began drawing. "Around the building in a semicircle. So you can reach in and take one while you admire our Blakely cupcakely creation!"

"How do we decorate the cupcakes?" Whitney asked. "How about edible glitter?"

"Glitter is always good," Kylie said. "But I think these cupcakes also need to say something."

"Congratulations? Happy graduation? We're outta here? *Adiós?*" Jenna suggested.

"How about 'Blakely Forever?'" Brynn suddenly spoke up.

"We could do the Blakely logo and write '4-ever' across it," Lexi said, trying to visualize it. "I think it'll work."

"I think it will work *really* well," said a voice, entering the teachers' lounge. It was Juliette. "I had to get a sneak peek of what PLC was doing for its grand finale."

"You make it sound like we'll never bake cupcakes again," Kylie said. "This isn't the end of the cupcake club."

"Yeah," Brynn said. "PLC forever!"

Juliette held up her hands. "Okay, okay. I can see you have things under control here."

Kylie looked around the kitchen. She was proud of the juniors and her original club. They had all bonded and were working together seamlessly. Juliette took her aside and asked gently, "Have you given your graduation speech some more thought?"

With all the baking and planning, Kylie had almost forgotten about the speech. "I, um, I don't even have it anymore. I threw it away."

"No, you didn't," Brynn said, eavesdropping on their conversation. "You put it in your pocket when I found it in the PLC binder."

"Good memory!" Juliette told the little girl.

"Oh, that's nothing!" Brynn said. "I remember everything Kylie wrote, word for word."

"You don't say." Juliette grinned. "Care to share it?"

"No!" Kylie exclaimed. "It's silly. I don't want anyone to hear it."

Brynn ignored her and began reciting from memory: "Take one cup of courage. You'll need it for the next few years to get through the moments when you doubt yourself. Add a pinch of creativity, a spoonful of stick-to-itiveness, and a heap of passion and purpose to guide you when there are no other directions to follow…"

"Stop!" Kylie begged her. But it was too late. Everyone in the lounge had overheard and was now gathered around them.

"What kind of recipe is *that*?" Whitney asked.

"Kylie's Recipe for Success," Brynn reported.

"In school and in life," Juliette said, smiling broadly. "Those are very wise words, Kylie."

"It makes me cry," Lexi said, tearing up. "Oh, Kylie. You have to read that at graduation."

"Is there more?" Jenna asked. "*Es brillante, chica.*"

"Yes…no. I dunno," Kylie said.

"Oh, there is!" Brynn insisted. "A lot more."

Kylie put her hand over the child's mouth. "I can take it from here, Brynn." She pulled a crumpled sheet of paper out of her jacket pocket and cleared her throat. She shot Jenna a look. "No laughing," she warned her. Then she began to read:

"Stir it up with a group of friends that love you for *you*—just being you, even if you're different or weird or stand out. Pour in people who believe in your ability to change the world, one cupcake at a time. Then sprinkle it with fun—because that's what makes everything sweeter. Even the mess and the mistakes and the burned batches. Oh, and the ones that taste lumpy or bitter! There are tons of those! You can get through all that if you remember the secret ingredient is fun. Fun fixes everything! Let your recipe cool, then share it. Spread the word like you spread frosting on a cupcake. And watch your cupcake rise and your business grow and your dreams take shape."

When she looked up, she saw Juliette was dabbing her eyes with a paper towel.

"Oh my, Kylie. That is simply beautiful."

"It is?" Kylie said. "I was really just writing it for myself…kind of a recipe for how I got through the tough times in elementary school and found PLC." But saying the words out loud, Kylie had to admit she felt something strange—a twinge of sadness that hadn't been there before. Maybe she would miss Blakely more than she thought. Maybe it had meant much more than she was allowing herself to acknowledge.

Jenna walked over and threw her arms around Kylie. "You're reading it at graduation. *Me escuchas?* Do you hear me?"

Sadie nodded. "Seriously, Kylie, I'm all choked up… and just look at Delaney and Lexi!" The pair was sobbing on each other's shoulders.

Nathaniel tugged on Kylie's sleeve. "I know sometimes it's hard to get up in front of a crowd and talk," he said. "But you *should* do it. Trust me."

Kylie took a deep breath. "Well, I guess I'm outvoted. I'll read my recipe at graduation."

"Hooray!" the entire group shouted.

Kylie put her arm around Brynn. "Thank you," she said.

"For what?" Brynn asked. "My photogenic memory?"

"For being a good friend and teaching your teacher a few things! And for being a great cupcake club leader."

Brynn looked surprised. "Leader?"

Kylie picked up a wooden spoon and gently rested it on

the little girl's head. "I hereby appoint Brynn Jasen president of PLC Jr. All in favor say 'Sprinkles!'"

"Sprinkles!" everyone shouted.

"I expect you to do great things with this club, and by the time you graduate in four years, you'll have trained a whole new group of PLCers who know how to bake, frost, and fix cupcake catastrophes," Kylie added.

"That's my specialty," Brynn said, beaming.

"Making them or fixing them?" Jenna teased.

Brynn scratched her head. "Both!"

Team Effort

When the day of graduation finally arrived, Kylie hadn't expected to feel so emotional. But there she sat on the edge of her bed, struggling to keep the tears from streaming down her cheeks. Graduation had seemed so far away, and now here she was, preparing to put on her cap and gown and start a whole new chapter of her life. How had it snuck up on her so fast? And how was it possible that Blakely and all the people there would never be part of her life again?

"You ready, Kylie?" her dad called upstairs. "We don't want to be late for the big day."

"Coming!" she shouted down. She shook off the sadness and smoothed her hair and took one last look in the mirror. She loved how her white lace graduation dress hung delicately off her shoulders.

"Your dad and I thought your outfit needed a little

something," Mrs. Carson said, appearing at Kylie's door with a velvet box. "Open it."

Kylie opened the box to reveal a tiny diamond cupcake charm on a gold chain. It was dotted with ruby, sapphire, and emerald "sprinkles." "Oh!" she gasped. "It's beautiful!"

Her mom helped her fasten the clasp, then took a step back to look at her daughter.

"When did you get to be so grown up?" she asked with tears in her eyes. "Our little Smiley Kylie is graduating."

"Oh, Mom, not you too," Kylie said, hugging her. "I'm trying to remember it's a happy day, not a sad one."

"I know. I know," her mom said. "But I have a pack of tissues in my purse, just in case."

Kylie's phone rang, and she was grateful for the distraction. "Sadie!" she said, picking it up. "Did you and your dad deliver the cupcakes to the school?"

"We have a problem," Sadie said. Kylie could hear the panic in her friend's voice. "How soon can you get here?"

"We're leaving now. Where will I find you?"

"Oh, trust me. You can't miss us."

When her parents pulled up in front of the school, Kylie saw what Sadie had meant. There, standing in front of the school's big, red doors, was their cupcake display under a tarp, going nowhere.

"It won't fit through the door," Sadie told her. She was dressed in a pretty navy-blue sundress and small heels that made her look even taller. "We've tried every angle. It's about an inch too big all around. What do we do?"

"Can we take the doors off?" Kylie asked Mr. Harris. "Or shave down the sides of the platform?"

"I don't have the tools with me," he said. "And there's no time to go home and get them. Besides, everyone's arriving." He pointed to cars pouring into the parking lot. Families began pushing past them to enter the building.

"I thought we measured it," Kylie said to Sadie. "So we wouldn't have this issue."

"We did. I sent the juniors to get the measurements. They were close…just off by an inch or two."

Kylie sent a group text: Major cupcake 911 at Blakely! All PLC members needed NOW!

Jenna had just arrived with her entire family. She was dressed in one of her mom's designs, a beautiful, billowy blue dress with puffy sleeves. Kylie thought she looked like

91

Cinderella—right down to her clear plastic pumps that resembled glass slippers. "*Vámanos!*" she said, directing her parents and siblings into the school ahead of her. "Mami, get good seats so you can see me get my diploma."

She raced to Kylie's side. "*Qué pasa?* Why are we outside instead of in?"

"The cupcakes won't fit through the door," Sadie repeated.

"This is not good," Lexi said, spotting her friends gathered around the intricate cupcake structure. Her graduation dress was a delicate pink floral print with a high-low hemline. "It's eighty degrees. All the frosting will melt if we don't get it inside!"

"Easier said than done," Mr. Harris said. "The only solution is to take everything off and carry it in by hand."

"Carry five hundred cupcakes—and a giant Blakely made out of 1,500 minis—into the school before graduation starts?" Kylie felt like banging her head against the red double doors. This wasn't happening...it couldn't be.

"We need to call in the troops," Delaney said. She was excited to be in the audience and watch her friends graduate. She hadn't thought she'd be assembling an army! "We need everyone—the juniors, Juliette, Herbie."

Kylie suddenly had an idea. "We need to call in more

hands than that!" She bolted into the school and up the stairs to Principal Fontina's office. She found her greeting parents in the rotunda.

"I need to make an announcement over the loud-speaker," Kylie shouted. "It's an emergency."

"What kind of an emergency?" Principal Fontina asked.

"I need the whole fifth grade to come help us carry cupcakes inside," Kylie said. "Two thousand of them."

Her principal's jaw dropped. "Now? On graduation morning?"

"Please!" Kylie pleaded with her. "It will move fast if we all work together and form an assembly line."

"Fine. You wait outside. I'll have the kids line up. But make it quick!"

"Trust me," Kylie assured her. "If our display is outside much longer, we're going to be serving cupcake soup at the reception!"

Juliette and Herbie held open the doors as the fifth graders lined up down the long Blakely hallway. "Everyone grab two cupcakes—carefully!" Herbie warned them. "Don't drop them or squeeze them or bump into anything. Just put them down on a table in the cafeteria, and come back for more."

Juliette smiled. "You've become quite the cupcake coach," she said. "I'm proud of you, little brother."

Brynn and the juniors had received the 911 and had finally arrived on the scene. "Oh, thank goodness!" Kylie said when she spotted them coming toward the front doors. "We need you to help us carry our Blakely inside Blakely."

"It weighs a ton!" Clementine pointed out. "Can't we roll it in?"

"The display we built won't fit," Sadie said. "We have to lift it off the base and slowly carry it up the stairs and down the hall to the cafeteria."

"It'll get wrecked," Nathaniel pointed out. "The green grass frosting is already wilting, and if we try to move it…"

"You'll go to the teachers' lounge and get us some piping bags filled with green frosting," Lexi instructed him. "You'll have to mix it up from scratch. And some red frosting—and white piping, while you're at it. Oh, and some gum glue and water in case you need to glue stuff back."

Brynn gulped. "You're trusting us in the teachers' lounge? By ourselves? Are you sure?"

Kylie looked at her watch. "We don't have a choice. The ceremony starts in ten minutes. PLC Jr. will have to handle the graduation cupcakes."

Together, they carried the cupcake structure inside, leaving frosting and minis in their path. "We're losing part of the roof!" Roxy screamed, grabbing several silver-dusted minis as they toppled off. "This is crazy!"

When they finally got the structure to the cafeteria, they saw that several of the minis had slipped off the front of the building—and the fondant flagpole they'd created was bent in half.

"Fix it!" Kylie said, grabbing Brynn by the shoulders. "You're the president. I'm trusting you to make this work. The ceremony is two hours long. Budget your time accordingly."

"Two hours? We can't fix this mess in two hours!" Nathaniel cried. "It took us two days to build it."

Brynn clapped her hands, summoning the group to attention. "Whitney and Clementine, you go mix up the new buttercream. Check my notebook. I wrote down how many drops of food coloring we used to make the frosting colors."

"Oh, thank goodness," Lexi said. "It has to match perfectly." She looked Nathaniel in the eyes. "Do not let me down."

"Reassemble the cupcakes in a semicircle around the mini Blakely building once they get it repaired," Jenna instructed Roxy. "Every cupcake needs to look and taste *perfecto*."

Sadie pointed to the clock on the cafeteria wall. "Guys, the ceremony is starting. We have to go."

Kylie took one last look at their mini-me's, already in action. "Break an egg!" she called after them. "That's cupcake-speak for good luck, you guys!"

Pomp and Circumstance

The graduation ceremony was quite a production, thanks to Juliette. The fifth grade sang three songs: Kelly Clarkson's "A Moment Like This," the Beatles' "Here Comes the Sun," and Miley Cyrus's "The Climb." Lexi had a solo in the last one: "I can almost see it—that dream I'm dreamin'."

When the class returned to their seats, Kylie leaned over and hugged Lexi. "You are such a great singer," she said. "I'm so glad you found your voice here at Blakely."

Lexi's eyes welled up. "Thanks to you and PLC," she said.

Both Jenna and Sadie were called onstage to read orations that Juliette had selected. Jenna's was a Spanish poem called "*Hay un lugar especial en mi corazón.*"

"What does that mean?" Kylie asked when Jenna sat back down.

"It means there's a special place in my heart," Jenna translated. "For Blakely and for all of you guys."

Sadie's reading was a quote by New England Patriots head coach Bill Belichick: "On a team, it's not the strength of the individual players, but the strength of the unit and how they all function together."

"When I read that quote, I thought of us," Sadie told her cupcake clubmates. "Together, we're unbeatable."

Finally, it was time for Meredith and Kylie to give their commencement addresses.

"I have learned a great deal during my time at Blakely," Meredith began. "I've learned about responsibility…what it means to have people follow you, worship you, and want to be you."

Jenna groaned. "Oh boy, here she goes."

Meredith looked over at Kylie, who was standing beside her at the podium. She paused for a moment, took a deep breath, and continued. "Someone I admire is the great actress Meryl Streep. And Meryl said, 'The formula of happiness and success is just being yourself in the most vivid way that you can.'"

Kylie gulped. Was Meredith talking to her? It sure sounded like an apology for all the mean things Meredith had done and said to her in the past.

"So in closing, I just want to say 'Do you!' Don't worry if people don't get it at first. Sometimes it takes time. But Meryl and I see the potential."

The audience erupted in thunderous applause. Lexi, Sadie, and Jenna could barely believe what they'd just heard.

"Well, that was unexpected," Lexi said. "Maybe Meredith is finally growing up."

"Maybe she's feeling sentimental," Sadie suggested.

"Maybe she hit her head and has amnesia," Jenna joked.

Next, Kylie took her spot at the podium. She read her recipe for success, then added a few words that weren't on the paper in front of her. She took a deep breath and spoke from the heart: "When I came to Blakely, I was the new kid. I didn't know anyone. I felt like an outsider. But you became my family." She felt the tears stinging the corners of her eyes. "I'll miss this school and all of you each and every day. No matter where the future takes me, you're part of me."

At the end of her speech, everyone in the auditorium stood and cheered. Mrs. Carson handed Ms. Shottlan a tissue, and Juliette hugged Kylie so tightly she could barely breathe.

"Have I told you how proud I am of you?" she asked her prize pupil.

"I'm proud of myself," Kylie said. "I did it."

"I never had a doubt," Juliette said. "Not from the moment I met you, Kylie Carson. Just knowing you has made my life sweeter than a cupcake."

"Oh my gosh!" Kylie suddenly remembered. "The graduation cupcakes! I left the juniors in charge!"

"Then let me give you your diploma so you can go check on them," Principal Fontina said. "It's alphabetical order…lucky that your last name starts with a *C*!"

She took the podium. "I would like to congratulate all our graduates today and hand out some certificates of achievement with your diplomas." She called a few names before Kylie heard hers. "Kylie Carson," Principal Fontina said. "We would like to acknowledge you as Student Most Likely to Succeed."

Juliette gave Kylie a little shove, and she went up to receive her award. "No pressure," Principal Fontina joked. "But we're all expecting great things from you."

Kylie looked out in the audience. She saw her parents, her teachers, and her cupcake club smiling and clapping. She thought starting PLC had been the greatest moment of her life so far—but this came in a close second.

When Kylie reached the cafeteria, the juniors had already re-piped and reassembled the entire display. All that was left to do was line the cupcakes in a perfect semicircle around it.

"Does it look okay?" Brynn asked nervously, seeing Kylie come through the cafeteria door.

"It looks more than okay. It's perfect," Kylie said. "Really. We couldn't have done any better ourselves."

Nathaniel was covered head to toe in frosting. "I have never piped so fast in my life!"

Roxy counted to make sure all the cupcakes had made it back onto the platform. "I get five hundred and five cupcakes," she told Brynn. "I counted twice."

"Oh, that's because I always make extras," Brynn said. "Just in case."

"It's just enough," Kylie said.

"Enough? For what?" Brynn asked.

"For each of the juniors to taste the sweet reward of their hard work." She handed one to Roxy. "Go ahead. Take a bite."

Roxy smiled and almost gobbled the cupcake whole. "A cupcake inside a cupcake inside my tummy," she said. "Yum."

"Double yum," Whitney said, peeling back a wrapper. "Who knew cupcakes taste so much better when you make them yourself?"

Nathaniel simply licked some of the icing off his fingers. "I feel like a cupcake," he said. "I'm frosted."

"You look like a cupcake," Clementine teased. She tossed him a cupcake, and he caught it in one hand.

"Hey!" she said. "You might have the makings of a really good juggler!"

"And you have the makings of a really great president," Kylie told Brynn. "You kept a cool head and stayed organized."

"Is that what you do?" Brynn asked.

"Well, I try. I've had my moments of panic."

"Like with your graduation speech?" Brynn said.

"Yeah. But I got through it…with a little help from my friends. And that includes all of you."

Brynn smiled. "I'm your friend? Really?"

"Always," Kylie said.

They heard the crowds pouring out of the auditorium and heading for the reception. Principal Fontina was the first one through the door. "Is that Blakely? Made out of cupcakes?" she asked, amazed.

"It is," Kylie said proudly. "It was Nathaniel's idea."

The boy looked at his shoes and blushed.

"Well, I can see our cupcake club is in very good hands for next year," Principal Fontina said, commending the juniors. "You chose your successors well, Kylie."

Jenna, Sadie, Lexi, and Delaney joined their BFF—but by the time they got to the cafeteria, almost all of the five hundred cupcakes had been devoured.

"I saved you one," Roxy told Jenna. "I thought you'd be hungry after the ceremony."

Jenna hugged her. "*Muchas gracias!*" she said.

"The juniors did it," Delaney said in disbelief. "I can't believe it, but they did."

"I can't believe this is our very last day at Blakely." Lexi began to tear up again. "We'll never walk through those big, red doors again!"

"I hate those big, red doors," Sadie said. "They almost ruined our cupcakes this morning."

"I love them." Kylie considered. "I love Blakely, and I love all you guys." Now it was her time to get teary as she drew her friends into a group hug.

"Well, it's a good thing we named the club Peace, Love, and Cupcakes, then," Jenna pointed out. "There's a lotta love goin' on here."

Kylie looked around the cafeteria. Everyone she had come to know in the past two years was gathered there. It felt surreal—like this was all a dream, and tomorrow she'd wake up again and attend her fifth grade classes. But fifth grade was over; Blakely was over.

Lexi read her mind. "Don't be sad," she said, squeezing Kylie's hand. "PLC forever, remember?"

Kylie touched the cupcake charm around her neck.

Forever and ever, she thought.

Confetti Circus Cupcakes with Rainbow Swirl Frosting

Confetti Circus Cupcakes

Makes 12 cupcakes

- 1 ⅔ cups flour
- ½ teaspoon baking powder
- ¼ teaspoon baking soda
- ½ teaspoon salt
- ½ cup (1 stick) unsalted butter, melted
- 1 cup sugar
- 1 egg
- ¼ cup sour cream
- ¾ cup milk
- 2 teaspoons vanilla extract
- ½ cup rainbow sprinkles

Directions

1. Have a grown-up help you preheat the oven to 350°F. Line a muffin tin with 12 cupcake liners. Since this

is a rainbow-riffic recipe, I chose 12 that were each a different color of the rainbow: red, orange, yellow, green, blue, purple—then repeat!

2. In a medium bowl, mix together the flour, baking powder, baking soda, and salt. Set aside.

3. Place the stick of butter in a large microwave-safe bowl, and microwave for about 30–45 seconds (depending on how cold the butter was in the first place).

4. Add the sugar to the large bowl and whisk. This butter-sugar mixture will be gritty. Let it cool in fridge for about two minutes.

5. Stir in egg, sour cream, milk, and vanilla extract until combined.

6. Slowly mix in the dry ingredients until the batter is thick but smooth. No lumps please!

7. Slowly stir in the rainbow sprinkles, but be careful not to overmix. The sprinkles will start to bleed their colors if you stir too much.

8. Fill each of the cupcake liners ⅔ full and bake for 18–22 minutes or until a toothpick inserted in the center comes out clean.

9. Have a grown-up remove from the oven, and let the cupcakes cool for 15 minutes before frosting.

Rainbow Swirl Frosting

1 cup (2 sticks) unsalted butter, softened

3 cups confectioners' sugar

¼ cup half-and-half

2 teaspoons vanilla extract

blue food coloring

pink food coloring

yellow food coloring

Directions

1. In the bowl of an electric mixer, using the paddle attachment, cream the softened butter and confectioners' sugar together until the mixture is light and fluffy.

2. Scrape the bowl, then add the half-and-half and vanilla extract, mixing on low for 1 minute then increasing to high until the frosting is creamy and smooth. Add a bit more powdered sugar if it seems too thin or dot more cream if too thick.

3. Divide the frosting into three small bowls. Add food coloring to the frosting. You decide how light or dark you like the colors to be.

4. Spoon a bit of each color into a piping back fitted

with a swirl tip. Pipe away! You can also top your frosting with a few rainbow sprinkles if you like!

Cupcake in a Cupcake

Cupcakes
Makes 12 cupcakes

- 2 dozen miniature cupcakes, either homemade or bought, with frosting on top, and chilled for at least an hour in the fridge
- 1 ½ sticks unsalted butter, softened
- 2 eggs
- 1 cup sugar
- 1 teaspoon vanilla
- 1 cup cake flour
- 1 teaspoon baking powder
- ¼ teaspoon salt
- ½ cup milk

Directions
1. Have a grown-up help you preheat the oven to 350°F. Line a muffin tin with 12 cupcake liners.

2. Remove and set aside your mini cupcakes from the fridge. Peel off their liners if they have them.

3. In the large bowl of an electric mixer, beat together the butter, eggs, sugar, and vanilla until combined.

4. In a separate bowl, whisk together the flour, baking powder, and salt.

5. Add the flour mixture and milk to the ingredients in the mixer, alternating between each addition. Beat until smooth, but don't overmix!

6. Fill each cupcake liner halfway to the top with batter. Place the mini cupcake in the center of the liner, and pour a little more batter on top of it, just to cover the mini. Place in the muffin tin on top of a cookie sheet to prevent it from spilling over.

7. Bake for approximately 20–25 minutes until the top of the cupcake is light golden brown.

8. Have a grown-up remove from the oven, and let the cupcakes cool for 15 minutes before frosting. Personally, I like a rich chocolate buttercream on these (see recipe below), but you could also compliment your mini flavors. For example, if you have a peanut butter mini, you could do peanut butter frosting on top of the whole cupcake.

Chocolate Buttercream Frosting

6 tablespoons butter, softened

3 cups confectioners' sugar

½ cup cocoa powder

⅓ cup milk

1 ½ teaspoon vanilla extract

Directions

1. Place butter in the bowl of an electric mixer and beat until creamy.

2. Add sugar and cocoa powder to the bowl, mixing well.

3. With the mixer on medium, beat in milk in small portions.

4. Add vanilla to the mixture. Beat on medium-high until frosting is creamy and smooth.

5. Spread on top of each cupcake with a knife or spatula, or swirl on top using a piping bag and tip. Shh! Don't tell anyone the surprise inside each cupcake! Let them take a bite and find it for themselves.

Carrie's Tips for Starting Your Own Cupcake Club

I get asked all the time by fans of our book series, "How do I do start a baking club in my school?" It's not as hard as you might think. All it requires are a few ingredients:

Step 1: Brainstorm Ideas

- Think about what you want your club to be and do. Will it focus on cupcakes or will you bake other sweet treats as well?
- What will you call your club?
- What will you do at every meeting?
- Where and when will your club meet?
- What is the goal of your club? To learn how to be a better baker, to raise funds for a charity through bake sales, or to hang out with other people who share your culinary passions?
- Who can join the club? Is it open to all ages or only certain grades?

- What adult (teacher, parent, coach, etc.) can help and advise you?

Step 2: Talk to the People in Charge

- Find out the person who approves new clubs in your school. Is it the principal, assistant principal, or a teacher? Make an appointment to speak to him/her and discuss what you would like to do. Be organized and ready to answer questions!

- Ask if there are any specific rules that your club must follow. Are you responsible for cleaning up after you bake? Do you need to get all announcements and events approved in advance?

- Make sure there is not a similar club already operating at your school. If there is, it can take away from your membership.

Step 3: Spread the Word!

- Create some colorful posters and flyers to advertise your new club and recruit members. Personally, I'd include a photo of a scrumptious, mouth-watering cupcake on mine (*that* will get people interested) and a catchy slogan: "Like to bake? SWEET! Join the Cupcake Club!" Include when the club will meet and where.

- Ask if you can speak to your peers as a group at assembly or during recess or lunch periods. Going classroom-to-classroom is a great way to reach kids as well.

- Create an email (your parent's is okay) so people can contact you with any questions and you can share club news. Start a list of members' emails/ phone numbers/classes so you can reach out to them as well.

Step 4: Divide and Conquer

- Organize your club into positions/offices so everyone has a responsibility. If you're starting the club, you may want to be president or copresident. You might also want a vice president (second in command), secretary (keeper of all notes), and treasurer (the person who keeps track of money).

- Be fair when assigning these jobs. Everyone who has an office should be dedicated to making the club the best it can be. Who will purchase ingredients? Who will be in charge of researching recipes? Can someone bring in a mixer and bowls from home?

Step 5: Consider Your Budget

- To keep your club running, you'll need to make sure you know what your operating costs will be. Some schools provide clubs with a small stipend every year. Others don't, and you might need to charge members a fee to participate.

- Take into account your grocery lists (ingredients can be pricey!), any equipment you might need, cookbooks, aprons, muffin pans, cupcake liners, even printing costs for making flyers to advertise your bake sales. Keep a tab of how much things cost and how much you are spending.

Step 6: Make Some Plans

- Look at your calendar and put down some possible dates for meetings, fund-raisers (bake sales!), guest speakers (maybe a local baker!), and excursions (visiting a local cupcakery).

- Hold your first bake! It's a good idea to start with the basics: a perfect vanilla and chocolate cupcake from scratch and a light and fluffy buttercream frosting. Once you get those down, you can add more complicated recipes to your repertoire and get fancy with the decorating.

Finally, don't forget to have fun! And don't try to bite off more than you can chew (pun intended!). Start small and build as you go along. You'll have the recipe for success in no time!

Acknowledgments

Thank you to everyone who has made The Cupcake Club such a sweet success and a LONG series—twelve books! We can't believe how far Kylie and company have come! Writing this last one has been bittersweet, but we've loved every minute of the journey.

Sourcebooks, you believed in us from Day 1 and helped us create such wonderful adventures for our Cupcake Club. Thank you, Steve, Kate, Elizabeth, Alex, and the rest of the gang. We will miss you (and might have to bring cupcakes by the office now and then).

Our families, the Berks, the Kahns, and the Saps: thank you for the endless love and support.

All the people who have believe in the power of PLC and have worked with such passion to help us bring it to the stage (can't wait for the new version of the musical to have its debut at NYMF Summer 2017 off-Broadway!). Jill Jaysen and the Center Stage kids, Rick Hip-Flores,

Rommy Sandhu, Liz Racanelli, David Madore, Louisa Pough, Lisa Dozier King, Matt Loehr, our brilliantly talented cast (Maddy, David, Calli, Alexa, Eliza, Diego, Jack, James, Casey, Miranda Jo, Merin, Ksenia, Victoria, Chloe, Jamilah, Grace, Cam, and Tai) and our hardworking crew on the NYMF production—we are so grateful to all of you. You have embraced this story and helped make a difference. (Guys, this is just the beginning!) Bravo one and all! Many thanks to Michelle Shapiro, Erik Stangvik, and NoBully.org; we are proud to have *Peace, Love, and Cupcakes: The Musical* align with your organization's goals to spread empathy and student compassion and eliminate bullying and cyberbullying in schools.

Finally, hugs and sprinkles to all our readers—you have kept us going all these years, asking for more stories and recipes and sharing your enthusiasm. You have inspired *us*. We hope you continue to bake and dream big! XO, Sheryl and Carrie

About the Authors

Sheryl Berk is the *New York Times* bestselling coauthor of *Soul Surfer*. An entertainment editor and journalist, she has written dozens of books with celebrities, including Britney Spears, Maddie Ziegler, and Zendaya. Her daughter, Carrie Berk, is a renowned cupcake connoisseur and blogger (facebook.com/PLCCupcakeClub; Instagram @plccupcakeclub) with more than 100,000 followers at the tender young age of twelve! Carrie cooked up the idea for the Cupcake Club series while in second grade. To date, she and Sheryl have written fifteen books together (with many more in the works!). *Peace, Love, and Cupcakes* had its world premiere as a delicious new musical at New York City's Vital Theatre in 2014. The Berk ladies are also hard at work on a new book series (Ask Emily) and several new plays, not to mention a worldwide movement based on PLC to empower kids to make a difference.

Peace Love and Cupcakes

$\mathcal{M}$eet Kylie Carson.

She's a fourth grader with a big problem. How will she make friends at her new school? Should she tell her classmates she loves monster movies? Forget it. Play the part of a turnip in the school play? Disaster! Then Kylie comes up with a delicious idea: What if she starts a cupcake club?

Soon Kylie's club is spinning out tasty treats with the help of her fellow bakers and new friends. But when Meredith tries to sabotage the girls' big cupcake party, will it be the end of the cupcake club?

Book
1

Recipe For Trouble

Meet Lexi Poole.

To Lexi, a new school year means back to baking with her BFFs in the cupcake club. But the club president, Kylie, is mixing things up by inviting new members. And Lexi is in for a not-so-sweet surprise when she is cast in the school's production of *Romeo and Juliet*. If only she could be as confident onstage as she is in the kitchen. The icing on the cake: her secret crush is playing Romeo. Sounds like a recipe for trouble!

Can the girls' friendship stand the heat, or will the cupcake club go up in smoke?

Book
2

Winner Bakes All

Meet Sadie.

When she's not mixing it up on the basketball court, she's mixing the perfect batter with her friends in the cupcake club. Sadie's definitely no stranger to competition, but the oven mitts are off when the club is chosen to appear on *Battle of the Bakers*, the ultimate cupcake competition on TV. If the girls want a taste of sweet victory, they'll have to beat the very best bakers. But the real battle happens off camera when the club's baking business starts losing money. Long recipe short, no money for icing and sprinkles means no cupcake club.

With the clock ticking and the cameras rolling, will the club and their cupcakes rise to the occasion?

Book
3

Icing on the Cake

Meet Jenna.

She's the cupcake club's official taste tester, but the past few weeks have not been so sweet. Her mom just got engaged to Leo—who Jenna is sure is not "The One"—and Peace, Love, and Cupcakes has to bake the wedding cake. Jenna is ready to throw in the towel, especially when she hears the wedding will be in Las Vegas on Easter weekend, one of the most important holidays for the club's business!

Can Jenna and her friends handle their busy orders—and the Elvis impersonators—or will they have a cupcake meltdown?

Book
4

Baby Cakes

𝓜eet Delaney.

New cupcake club member Delaney is shocked to find out her mom is expecting twins! When her parents first tell her, the practical joker thinks they must be pulling her leg. For ten years she's had her parents—and her room—all to herself. She LIKED being an only child. But now she's going to be a big sis.

The girls of Peace, Love, and Cupcakes get together to bake cupcakes and discover Delaney is worried about what kind of a big sister she will be. She's never even babysat before! But her cupcake club friends rally to her side for a crash course in Big Sister 101.

Book

5

Royal Icing

$\mathcal{M}$eet Kylie.

As the founder and president of Peace, Love, and Cupcakes, Kylie's kept the club going through all kinds of sticky situations. But when PLC's adviser surprises the group with an impromptu trip to London, the rest of the group jumps on board—without even asking Kylie. All of sudden, Kylie's noticing the club doesn't need their president nearly as much as they used to. To top it off, the girls get an order for two thousand cupcakes from Lady Wakefield of Wilshire herself—to be presented in the shape of the London Bridge! Talk about a royal challenge...

Can Kylie figure out her place in the club in time to prevent their London Bridge—and PLC—from falling down?

Book
6

Sugar and Spice

Meet Lexi.

The girls of Peace, Love, and Cupcakes might be sugar and spice and everything nice, but the same can't be said for Meredith, whose favorite hobby is picking on Lexi. So when the PLC gets a cupcake order from the New England Shooting Starz—the beauty pageant Meredith is competing in—the girls have a genius idea: enter Lexi into the competition so she can show Meredith once and for all that she's no better than anyone else. Problem is, PLC has to make Lexi a pageant queen—and one thousand cupcakes—all in a matter of weeks!

Have the girls of Peace, Love, and Cupcakes bitten off more than they can chew?

Book

7

Sweet Victory

Meet Sadie.

MVP Sadie knows what it takes to win—both on the court and in the kitchen. But when Coach Walsh gets sick and has to temporarily leave school, Sadie's suddenly at a loss. What will she do without Coach's spot-on advice and uplifting encouragement? Luckily, Sadie's got Peace, Love, and Cupcakes on her side. Her friends know that the power of friendship—and cupcakes—might be just what Sadie needs! Together, they rally to whip up the largest batch of sweet treats they've ever made, all to help support Coach Walsh. When the going gets tough, a little PLC goes a long way. But this record-breaking order might just be too much for the club...

Can the girls pull it together in time to score a win for Sadie—and Coach Walsh?

Book

8

Bakers on Board

$\mathcal{M}$eet Jenna.

It's "anchors aweigh!" for the Cupcake Club!

Jenna's stepdad, Leo, is taking his family on a Caribbean cruise. Unfortunately, Jenna's younger siblings get the chicken pox, leaving Leo with four extra tickets. Enter Peace, Love, and Cupcakes! Leo says Jenna's four besties can come—in exchange for baking twelve thousand cupcakes for his company's pirate-themed event. Shiver me timbers, that's a lot of icing! Now pros the cupcake-baking game, PLC takes on the challenge.

But when a freak rainstorm flares up on the night of the big event, will it be rough seas for the girls?

Book

9

Vote for Cupcakes!

$\mathcal{M}$eet Delaney.

Cupcakes for the win!

When Delaney discovers there's been a cut to the art budget, she decides it's time to make a change! The race for class president is quickly approaching, and Delaney's going to run. Her besties in Peace, Love, and Cupcakes are ready to help in any way they can. But when Delaney's demands start infringing on PLC's ability to get out their orders—and the girls' friendships—things start to get out of hand. The girls aren't sure Delaney really knows what it takes to become president...or whether she's running for the right reasons.

As the election approaches, will it be Delaney for president? Or will her campaign (and PLC) crash and burn?

Book
10

Hugs and Sprinkles!

$\mathcal{M}$eet Lexi.

PLC is about to find out that secrets and crushes are a recipe for disaster...

The fifth graders at Blakely Elementary are having their very first dance! The girls of Peace, Love, and Cupcakes are all thrilled...except for Kylie, who confides in Lexi that she wishes she had a special someone to go with. Before long, notes and gifts show up in Kylie's locker from a "secret admirer" who seems to know her perfectly!

Kylie is over the moon—until the discovery of her admirer's identity leads to two feuding friends! Can PLC pull it together in time for the big dance?

Book
11